"Bailey, do me a favor..."

"Sure. What do you need?"

"Get up and slowly move over here with me," Sean said, never taking his eyes off the big, tawny-colored cat lying on a limb about twenty-five feet above Bailey's head.

"What are you looking at?" she asked as she walked over to stand beside him. He knew the moment she looked up and saw the mountain lion. "Oh, no! Sean, that's a—" Her words came to an abrupt halt when the animal opened its mouth and let loose with a scream.

When Bailey gave a startled cry and whirled around to run, he caught her by the arm. "Stay right beside me," he said in a low voice. "Running will make him want to chase after you. Just stay beside me and do what I tell you."

"O-okay."

"Crowley isn't our biggest threat right now." He made himself as big as he could, then nodded toward the limb as the lion raised itself to a crouch. *"He is."*

Kathie Ridings lives in her native southern Illinois on the land her family settled in 1839. A former teacher of tole folk-art painting, basket weaving and crochet, she's always loved to read. Now she plots her books while painting, weaving a basket or crocheting something warm to wear. Readers may contact Kathie by emailing kathieridings@gmail.com or find her on Facebook at Facebook.com/kathie-ridings-100209191904884.

Books by Kathie Ridings

Love Inspired Suspense

Wyoming Christmas Peril

WYOMING CHRISTMAS PERIL

KATHIE RIDINGS

LOVE INSPIRED SUSPENSE

INSPIRATIONAL ROMANCE

LOVE INSPIRED® SUSPENSE

INSPIRATIONAL ROMANCE

ISBN-13: 978-1-335-72280-5

Wyoming Christmas Peril

Copyright © 2021 by Kathie DeNosky

This edition published by arrangement with Harlequin Books S.A.

For questions and comments about the quality of this book, please contact us at CustomerService@Harlequin.com.

Love Inspired
22 Adelaide St. West, 40th Floor
Toronto, Ontario M5H 4E3, Canada
www.LoveInspired.com

Printed in U.S.A.

Have not I commanded thee? Be strong and of a good courage; be not afraid, neither be thou dismayed: for the Lord thy God is with thee whithersoever thou goest.
—*Joshua* 1:9

To Stacy Boyd and Tina James for believing in me
even in the times I doubt myself.

ONE

Perspiration beaded Bailey O'Keefe's forehead, and her body trembled all the way to her toes as she stared at the polished, blue-steel gun barrel aimed at the space between her eyebrows. There was so much that she still hadn't done in her short twenty-five years. She was supposed to have time for wonderful adventures, time to experience all sorts of amazing things in this new chapter of her life.

Instead, she was going to die without ever having hiked through a northwest forest in search of a Sasquatch, ridden a donkey to the bottom of the Grand Canyon or watched a Hawaiian volcano erupt. She'd never get to buy a new car, have a home of her own, or get married and have a family.

She was going to die. And all because she had agreed to switch her lunch break with her coworker, Mary Ann Miller. But that was probably for the best. Mary Ann had a husband and family who needed her and it would be devastating for her two little boys to lose their mother at Christmas. For the rest of their lives they would remember and grieve that they'd lost her at what should be a joyous time of year. Bailey didn't have anyone who would even miss her.

The ringing phone on the counter beside her brought her back to the present and when she looked up, her assailant's steely gray gaze pinned her in place. "I told you to answer that phone, honey." Clearly running out of patience, he sounded a lot like a growling animal when he spoke. His inappropriate familiarity and intimidating sneer made her skin crawl, especially when he tilted his head toward Earl McKenzie, the bank's security guard, lying facedown on the polished marble floor. "I'd hate to have to blow away you or Pops just because you went and did something stupid." She wouldn't have thought it was possible, but his menacing scowl darkened. "Now. Answer. That. Phone!"

"O-okay," Bailey stammered, forcing the word past her chattering teeth.

Dear Lord, please give me the courage

and strength to do whatever I have to in order to get myself and Earl out of this.

As she struggled to pull air into her lungs, she drew on the same determination she'd found when she'd discovered her mother's terminal illness had wiped them out financially and the bank had started foreclosure proceedings on the only home she'd ever known.

She had survived that—despite the best efforts of Mr. John Harmon, Senior Loan Officer at the Tristate Savings and Loan back in her hometown in Illinois. She'd survive this, as well.

And when she did make it to the other side of this fiasco, she fully intended to make a bucket list of everything she'd always wanted to do, but never had the courage to try. Then, one by one, she was going to check them off as she lived her life to the fullest.

She was going to camp out in the wilderness and gaze up at the endless stars filling the vast Wyoming night sky. She was going to feel the wind in her hair as she rode a horse across an open meadow. And one day—she hoped and prayed—she would find a good man she loved, who loved her in return, and they'd get married and have a beautiful family together.

She straightened her shoulders and drew herself up to her full five feet two inches. This horrible man was not going to take her dreams away from her. With the Lord's help, she was going to get herself and Earl out of this mess alive. But at the moment she had no idea how.

Held captive by his cold, heartless gaze, she slowly picked up the phone and held it up to her ear. "H-hello?"

"Bailey?"

"Yes."

"This is Sean Hanson. I'll be negotiating on behalf of the FBI today. How are you doing? Are you all right?"

The agent's smooth, rich baritone had a soothing effect on her frayed nerves and she fleetingly wondered how anyone's voice could be so calming. But when she noticed the bank robber glaring at her, his darkening expression sent a shiver racing up her spine and drove the tiny sliver of comfort away.

"All things considered, I'm okay. For now," she added cautiously.

"What about Mr. McKenzie?" the agent asked. "Is he all right, as well?"

"No. Not at all," Bailey said, fighting back

tears. Earl was such a nice old gentleman and she prayed he wasn't badly injured. "He's… lying on the floor and I'm pretty sure he's unconscious."

Poor Earl's only crime had been wearing new leather boots to work that day. If they hadn't squeaked with every step he took, he might have been successful at sneaking up behind the robber. But when the man heard Earl's approach, he'd swung around and conked the poor older man on the side of the head with his gun. Earl flailed his arms and tore the robber's mask from his face as he fell into a heap on the floor. He hadn't moved since.

"Is Mr. McKenzie breathing?" Sean asked, patiently.

"I-I think so." Bailey glanced over the counter at the unconscious man on the floor. When she heard Earl's soft snores, she breathed a shaky sigh of relief. "Y-yes, he's alive. But there's a lot of blood."

"Where is he injured?"

"He has a cut on his…right temple," she answered shakily.

"Take a deep breath, Bailey. I give you my word that I'll do everything possible to get you and Mr. McKenzie out of this," Sean promised. "But I need for you to stay calm and trust me. Do you think you can do that?"

Maybe it was the sound of his voice or his reassuring words that helped to restore some of her confidence. She wasn't sure. But she did believe Sean Hanson would do whatever he could to get her and Earl out of the situation safely.

Clearing her throat, she took a deep breath. "Yes, I can do that."

"Good. Now, tell the man holding you hostage that I need to talk to him."

Turning her attention to the man in front of her, she started to hand him the phone. "The agent wants to talk to you."

The robber shook his head. "Tell him I ain't talking to nobody until they pull back at least two blocks."

Bailey bit her bottom lip to keep it from quivering. The last thing she wanted was for Sean Hanson and the authorities to move farther away. But if cooperating got her even a tiny bit closer to being able to walk away from this, it would be worth it.

Taking a fortifying breath, she forced herself to nod and repeat what the man had said. "He won't talk to you or anyone else until everyone moves two blocks away."

"Tell him the only way we'll move back is

if he allows an ambulance crew inside to remove Mr. McKenzie for medical treatment," Sean countered, his tone patient but firm.

Bailey felt a moment of panic at the thought of being left completely alone with the bank robber. But she quickly tamped it down. Earl needed a doctor, as soon as possible. She, on the other hand, was still physically all right and she had faith that God would keep her that way.

"The agent said they will do what you want if you'll let them send paramedics in for Earl." She could tell the robber was weighing his options when he glanced down at the still-unconscious older man.

Shrugging, the robber finally muttered, "He ain't no good to me knocked out. Tell the cop they have to move back first. Then two medics can come in to get the old man. But they come in alone. Nobody else enters this building." He pushed the barrel of his gun closer to her forehead. "If they try, I'll shoot *you*."

His menacing grin convinced her he meant every word.

Bailey gazed back at the man. When he'd entered the bank, wearing a black mask and white cowboy hat, the man had looked more like the Lone Ranger than a bank robber.

But Tonto was nowhere in sight, and the silver bullets in the man's gun weren't just his calling cards—they were meant to send her and poor Earl to the Promised Land.

She took a deep breath and conveyed the robber's message. "He said to tell you to send in the ambulance crew, but no one else. H-he's going to…shoot me if you do."

"I won't let that happen, Bailey," Sean assured her. "Tell him to give us ten minutes to pull back and then we'll send in the paramedics. Once they are out and on their way to the hospital in Cheyenne, make it clear that I expect to speak directly to him. And no double crosses."

"Is there anything else?" she asked.

"No." He paused for a moment before he finished. "You're doing great, Bailey. Take a deep breath and hang tight. I meant it when I said I will do everything in my power to get you out of this safely."

"O-okay. Thank you."

She bit her lip to keep it from trembling as she hung up the phone. She hated losing Sean's calming presence, even if it was just over the phone. Now that he was going to be negotiating directly with the bank robber, all she could do was try to stay calm and pray he succeeded.

* * *

While Sean waited for the paramedics to stabilize the bank guard for transport, he re-read the FBI file on Harold Crowley, their bank robber. He and this creep had history, and Sean was determined it wasn't going to repeat itself. Even though Sean had officially resigned his position and had left the FBI behind, this case—this criminal—had haunted him. It was why the special agent in charge had pulled some strings to allow him to be here—he knew Sean needed some closure on this once and for all.

His jaw tightened. Five years ago banks started getting hit almost every month in Wyoming, Idaho or Montana, making state and local police, as well as the FBI, look like the Keystone Cops in their constantly failing efforts to stop the robber who was always dressed in a black domino mask, a white Resistol felt cowboy hat and black leather gloves. No one had ever been able to give authorities a description of him beyond his approximate height and weight, and because of the gloves, they'd never been able to get his fingerprints. Fortunately, as efficient as he had been at robbing banks, he hadn't harmed anyone—at least, not at first.

All that changed a little over eighteen

months into Crowley's tristate crime spree. Whether on purpose or by accident the teller had torn off his mask in her desperation to get away from him and something inside the man must have snapped. He'd murdered that poor woman, the mother of two little kids. During the getaway someone outside the bank had managed to take a picture with their cell phone, and the FBI had finally been able to identify the crook, but he disappeared for a few years and had only resumed his illegal undertakings last fall.

"The paramedics will be ready to transport to Cheyenne in five," Special Agent in Charge Sam Fowler advised, drawing Sean back to the present.

"I'll be ready." He needed to let the past stay right where it was and get up to speed on this creep's more recent criminal activities.

When Fowler's offer came in for Sean to take over a hostage negotiation at the bank in Eagle Fork, he'd thought his friend had to be joking. The small community had a population of just under five hundred people. The place barely qualified as more than a dot on a map. Aside from the small, family-owned bank, the town boasted a church, a café, a garage with a couple of gas pumps out front and the Rancher's General Store. Eagle Fork didn't even have a stoplight. To be honest, it didn't need one.

It really hadn't made any sense to Sean that a career criminal like Crowley would target a bank with such limited assets. But as he scanned the list of banks the man had allegedly hit since his reappearance last year, Sean couldn't find a single one associated with any of the national financial institutions. These days the man targeted *only* small, privately-owned hometown banks.

As he continued reading, his heart suddenly stalled. Crowley had killed two people recently—a female branch manager at the first part of the year in Idaho and a male bank customer. Both had seen his face and a profiler had made a note on the file that killing them had apparently been Crowley's way of punishing them for not following orders during the robbery.

Sean rubbed his hand over the tight muscles at the back of his neck and flattened his mouth into a grim line as the memory of Crowley's first victim came rushing forward. A pretty, dark-haired woman in her late twenties, she'd been a wife and the mother of two toddlers. She should have had her whole life in front of her. Instead, she'd found herself in the wrong place at the wrong time.

It was the same situation Bailey O'Keefe found herself in now.

He rarely prayed anymore—but he meant every word of his heartfelt prayer now. *God, please don't let this woman see Crowley without his mask.*

The paramedics had already gotten Mr. McKenzie out of harm's way, so Crowley must not see him as a threat. But Bailey? He needed to find out if she'd seen the man's face before he started the next phase of his negotiation. It was something that could mean the difference between life and death for her.

He turned his Bluetooth headset back on. As he signaled the FBI Mobile Command Center to put another call through to the bank, he concentrated on finding the right words to generate the best outcome.

"H-hello?" Bailey answered.

The sound of her soft voice caused his gut to clench. She was terrified and with good reason. His anger came to a full boil. She shouldn't be in this position, shouldn't be afraid that her life might come to an end today because of a piece of garbage like Crowley.

Sean stared at the bank building, calculating the distance and the time it would take to cover it. He wasn't nearly close enough to get to her in time to protect her if things suddenly went south.

"Are you doing okay, Bailey?"

"Y-yes." He could tell she wasn't, but he admired her determination to put up a brave front.

"Before you hand the phone over to the man holding you hostage, I'm going to ask you something and I don't want you to say anything but yes or no." He paced back and forth along the perimeter containment barrier as he posed the dreaded question. "Is he still wearing his mask?"

"No."

Sean clenched his teeth so hard he was surprised he didn't hear a couple of them crack. Determined not to let the tension he was feeling color the tone of his voice, he forced himself to sound calm when he was feeling anything but.

"Okay. Hang in there, Bailey. Now, hand the phone over to him and we'll see if we can get this ordeal over for you."

He heard a muffled exchange between Bailey and the robber before she came back on the line. "He said he'll only talk to you… through me."

Sean narrowed his eyes. He wasn't the least bit surprised that the robber had reneged on part of their earlier deal. One thing Crowley hadn't changed about his MO was the fact that he refused to speak to anyone in law enforcement. From all witness accounts, the man had good reason not to. His voice was reputed to be deep, raspy and *very* memorable. He could change his visual appearance by growing a beard or coloring his hair to try to fool law enforcement, but the sound of his voice was more difficult to disguise. The good thing about Crowley's refusal to talk to him was the fact that Sean could keep track of how Bailey was holding up under the pressure, as well as continue to encourage and reassure her.

"It's okay, Bailey. We're going to get through this." Staring down the street, Sean stopped pacing when he realized they had pulled back far enough for Crowley's view of them to be partially obstructed. The bank entrance was at the corner of the building, and the only windows on the west side were small and had fixed awnings over the top halves to block the glare of the afternoon sun. A grim smile tugged at the corners of his mouth as a plan began to take shape. "Trust me, Bailey. We can handle this."

Ten minutes later, after listening to her deliver Crowley's demands, Sean decided to stall the robber. He could use the time to outline his plan to the agents and various assisting police officers, then set up their positions to take the criminal down. "Tell him I'll see what I can do and call back when I have some answers for him."

"All…right," she said, sounding dejected. He knew Bailey had just about reached her breaking point. To her, his hanging up the phone probably felt like he was abandoning her.

He tried to make his voice as reassuring as possible. "I promise it won't take much longer to resolve this."

Ending the call, he turned to SAC Fowler and outlined his plan. "We'll only be able to move a handful of men into the blind spot, but if Crowley scopes things out before he exits the bank with Ms. O'Keefe, he'll see the rest of the men behind the barricade and won't realize that there are a few of us missing."

"He's going to think he can get away." Fowler nodded. "That will make it easier when they clear the door for you to move in and grab the hostage while the team and I take down Crowley."

"You're leading the team?" Sean asked. It was unusual for an SAC to take the lead, but not out of the question.

"I'd like to take this guy down the same as you," Sam answered.

Sean double-checked the service pistol in the holster on his utility belt, the one he'd had since his training days at Quantico, removed his wide-brimmed Resistol hat and sherpa-lined suede jacket to maximize his maneuverability, and adjusted the Velcro straps on his bulletproof vest. He took a deep, steadying breath as he put his coat and hat in one of the Bureau's cars and reached for his FBI ball cap. Pulling it down so the bill could shade his eyes, he was ready to get this thing over with and send Bailey O'Keefe home safe and sound.

As he and Fowler led the team of four agents and two federal marshals down an alley to another side street that would lead them straight to the west side of the bank building, Sean mentally went over his chances of getting Bailey out of Crowley's clutches. There was no margin for error. It was all or nothing. He had one shot at getting her out safely and if he failed, it would no doubt be deadly for her and most likely him, as well.

"No pressure, Hanson," he muttered under his breath.

When they reached the bank and moved into position, Sean and three members of the team found their way around the building to crouch on the south side of the double doors, while Fowler and the other three men waited on the west side. Turning on his Bluetooth, he gave the signal for the Mobile Command Center down the street to put the call through to the bank.

"Hello," Bailey answered, sounding exhausted.

"This is almost over, Bailey," he said, feeling the need to reassure her. "Tell the man he has a deal. In a couple of minutes an agent is going to park a car with a full tank of gas across the street. Once the robber leaves the bank, he's to let you go and drive away." He waited a moment before he added, "And tell him all deals are off if there's even a hint that he's about to double-cross us."

She repeated what he'd told her, then paused as she waited for Crowley's answer. "He said that wasn't the deal. He'll take me with him and release me when he knows he's in the clear."

Sean shook his head. "The deal changed when he went back on his word earlier about talking directly to me. Right now the deal stands as stated. If he wants to drive away from this, he has to release you first or the deal is off. After all, if he wants us to give him something, he has to give us something in return."

He knew that Crowley had no intention of letting Bailey go—not alive, anyway. But Sean had to sell the man on the idea he was going to pull off his escape. Otherwise, he wouldn't walk right into their trap. Crowley didn't have the slightest notion that he wasn't going to make it past the bank doors before he was taken into federal custody.

"He isn't happy, but he says all right."

The relief Sean detected in her voice caused his gut to clench. She didn't know and he couldn't tell her that the trickiest part of her release from this nightmare was yet to come. If things didn't go off without a hitch, she was very likely going to die and there wouldn't be a thing Sean could do to stop it.

TWO

When Bailey pushed open one of the two glass doors of the bank entrance, she saw that a car across Main Street was the only one parked along the three blocks that made up the downtown area of Eagle Fork. It had to be the one the FBI had left for her captor. It was so close, yet it seemed so far away. He'd told her he would release her when he got to the car. Oh how she wanted to believe him. But he'd lied about talking directly to the FBI agent and instead had made her act as the go-between every time Sean Hanson called. How could she trust him to be honest about letting her go?

"Stop dragging your feet and get moving," he growled close to her ear. His hot breath on her skin made her shudder and she feared she would be physically ill. When he pressed the barrel of the gun into her side, she cringed and forced herself to focus on walking forward one step at a time.

As the door to the bank swished shut behind her captor, it felt like bands of steel suddenly wrapped around her waist and jerked her away from the bank robber. This new man spun them around as he wrapped her tightly in his arms and pulled her to him, tucking her head securely against his chest. A split second later a shot rang out and she both heard and felt a groan from the man holding her. Together, they fell to the sidewalk before she could even process what had happened—that this man had been shot while protecting her. Now he lay limp and unmoving on top of her.

Sheer panic coursed through her. She screamed and began pushing at the body to get it off her. She heard a scuffle by the bank doors, but she didn't pay a lot of attention to what was going on. She couldn't. She had what must be a dead body on top of her and she wanted it off.

"Help! Please help!"

The man she had thought was dead startled her when he whispered close to her ear. "It's…all right, Bailey. It's…me. Sean Hanson." In her panicked state, it took her a moment to recognize his name and his voice.

He sounded as if it was difficult for him to breathe. But he wasn't dead, and hearing his warm baritone was like a balm to her jangled nerves. *Thank you, God, for saving this man's life.*

"Are you…okay?" She realized the foolishness of the question as soon as she asked it. He'd taken a bullet that had been meant for her. Of course he wasn't all right. Tears blurred her vision as she looked around. "I have to find someone to help you."

"Give me a second…to catch my breath." He untangled his legs from hers and rolled onto his back beside her.

She sat up and, pushing her hair away from her face, searched his torso. There were no visible bullet holes or blood that she could see. "Where were you shot?"

"My…back." He tried to sit up, but she pushed him back down on the sidewalk.

"You need to wait until the paramedics check your wounds before you get up." She gasped when he ignored her, and not only sat up, but slowly rose to his feet.

He winced when he gingerly rolled his shoulders. "Oh yeah, that's definitely gonna leave a mark." After releasing the Velcro straps on what she now recognized as body armor, he removed it then turned it around to the back to show her the mangled bullet embedded in the layers of fabric. "I'll admit that it hurts and it's probably going to feel worse tomorrow." She watched him study the back of the body armor. "And the FBI definitely owes me a new Kevlar vest, but otherwise, I'm doing okay." He smiled and held out his hand. When she placed her hand in his, he groaned and winced as he pulled her to her feet, but the strength of his grip did more than his words to convince her that he really was okay.

"I don't believe we've been officially introduced. I'm Sean Hanson." A tingling warmth streaked from her fingers all the way up to her shoulder when he enclosed her hand in both of his. "Even though it hasn't been under the best of circumstances, it's nice to meet you, Ms. O'Keefe."

Bailey felt her stomach flutter and her mouth become as dry as a desert when she looked up into his dark brown eyes. A good twelve inches taller than her petite five feet two inches, Sean Hanson looked like the quintessential cowboy from his wide shoulders and narrow waist all the way to his big, booted feet. With thick coffee-brown hair and a day or two growth of dark beard, he was handsome in a way that made it hard for her to draw in enough air.

"Bailey, are you hurt?" He was looking at her with concern and she realized she'd been staring at him like a love-struck teenager.

"Um, no. I'm fine." She shivered from the gusts of cold wind promising more snow. Embarrassed and needing to collect herself, she started toward the bank doors. "I think I'll go inside and get my coat and bag."

He placed his hand on her shoulder to stop her. "The Evidence Response Team has to process the crime scene before they let anyone back inside. But I'll tell them you need your personal belongings as soon as they've finished collecting what they need." He spoke to one of the agents going into the bank, then turned back to her. "You should be able to pick up your things at the sheriff's office later this evening after you've given your statement." He walked her over to one of the many government vehicles that had descended on Main Street in the past few minutes, reached inside to remove a heavy suede, sherpa-lined jacket and a wide-brimmed black hat. Smiling, he took his ball cap off, put the cowboy hat on and draped the jacket over her shoulders. "This should keep you warm until your coat is returned."

"Th-thank you, but won't you be cold without it?" The jacket was heavy, warm and smelled of leather, fresh air and Sean Hanson. It was like being wrapped in his arms all over again. As pleasant as the reminder was, it wasn't in her best interest to read anything into the gesture. He was just doing his job.

"I'm not likely to be cold for a while," he said, pulling the collar up around her neck. "I'm still running on a fair amount of adrenaline."

She started to tell him how much she appreciated his help and that she was fairly certain she owed him her life. But she stopped when the handcuffed man who'd held her hostage most of the day was led past her and Sean on the way to a police van.

"Better enjoy yourself while you can, little sister." The bank robber sneered and nodded his head toward Sean. "Your and your boyfriend's days are numbered. You'll both be dead long before I ever go to trial."

She gasped and stepped back at the venom in his raspy voice and the hatred in his eyes. A shiver ran the length of her spine that had nothing whatsoever to do with the biting cold of the early December afternoon.

Sean wrapped his arm around her shoulders and hugged her to his side as if trying to shield her from the ugliness of the man's threats. "Get him out of here," he ordered the marshals. As they led the criminal away, he shook his head. "Don't pay attention to anything he says, Bailey. He's in custody now and can't hurt you."

"Will he be in jail until the trial?" She shuddered at the thought of her captor being set free on bail for even a second. There was no doubt in her mind that if he was released, he'd kill her as soon as he could.

"I'm pretty sure they're going to want to keep him locked up. He's got a rap sheet as long as my arm and he's a definite flight risk." Sean's voice softened and he tightened his arm around her shoulders in a comforting gesture. "Trust me, he'll be going away for a long time. Probably the rest of his life."

"I'm telling myself that," she said, watching the marshals put the bank robber into the back of their van. "But my mind won't stop going over all the what-ifs."

"Hanson, I need you in Cheyenne as fast as you can get here," Sam Fowler said when Sean answered his phone.

Forcing himself to wake up, Sean threw back the covers, sat up on the side of his bed and flinched at the soreness that had stiffened the muscles in his back. He glanced at the clock on the bedside table. Whatever reason his friend had for calling him at two-thirty in the morning couldn't be good.

"What's going on, Sam?" he asked, dreading the answer.

"Crowley escaped."

The urgency of the two words was all it took for Sean to ignore the pain in his back and get to his feet to gather some clothes to throw on. "Have you sent somebody to pick up Ms. O'Keefe?"

He wasn't interested in hearing how the thug had managed to get away from two highly-trained lawmen. It really didn't matter. The bottom line was, Crowley was on the loose, which meant that Bailey O'Keefe was in imminent danger after he had promised her she would be safe. *God, please let the authorities get to her before Crowley.*

"Yeah, I contacted detectives from the highway patrol to pick her up and bring her to the federal building out by the airport." Sam paused a moment, then added, "And before you ask why I'm not using our agents or the US Marshal Service to bring her in—

I'm pretty sure we have a leak here in the office."

"That explains the highway patrol, but what makes you think there's a leak?" Sean clamped the phone between his ear and shoulder as he pulled on a pair of jeans, then reached in the closet for a chambray shirt.

"Instead of interrogating Crowley here, the Denver field office insisted on having him transferred to a detention center down there. Only eight or nine people knew he was being transported tonight by car instead of flying him down there in the morning. And every one of them was from this office or the US Marshals office." Sam sounded like the weight of the world rested squarely on his shoulders. "Anyway, that's not your problem. I wouldn't have bothered you, but you have more experience with this perp than just about anyone else, and I know how much bringing Crowley to justice means to you. I figured you'd want to be in on this."

"You got that right." Sean fastened the snaps on the front of his shirt in record time, stuffed the tail into the waistband of his jeans, then grabbed his wallet and keys from the dresser. Figuring a damaged Kevlar vest was better than no vest at all, he put it on, buckled his utility belt with his holstered sidearm around his waist and ran downstairs to the mudroom. After quickly shoving his arms into his coat and tugging on his boots, he left the house and broke into a run as he crossed the yard to the hangar where he kept his helicopter. "I'll be there in less than thirty minutes. Make sure somebody's at the airport to meet me. I'll let you know when I'm in the air."

"Copy that," Sam said, ending the call.

A little less than thirty minutes later, Sean eased his helicopter down onto the tarmac at the Cheyenne airport next to the Phillips Freight hangar. Jackson Phillips, the owner of the air freight service, had been friends with the Hanson family for over fifty years. As one of the benefits of that relationship, there was always space available for Sean to leave his chopper inside the heated hangar whenever he had to be in Cheyenne. Sean got the night guard to help him push the helicopter into the building, and by the time the hangar door came down, Sam had arrived to drive him to the federal building just down the road.

"I got a call from one of the state troopers on my way to get you," Sam said as soon as Sean got into the car. "They picked up Ms.

O'Keefe and should arrive at the office about the same time we do."

"Since there's a breach in security, I assume all of the safe houses are out of the question." Sean secured his shoulder belt as Sam drove away from the hangar. "So what's plan B?"

"You."

"Me?" Sean couldn't believe his friend was serious. For one thing, he'd resigned his position with the Bureau three years ago and was no longer considered an insider. Federal government law enforcement agencies were extremely territorial about who guarded their witnesses. In their view, they didn't want or need help doing their job, especially from someone no longer in their ranks.

Sam nodded. "Until I figure out who's leaking information and who it's being leaked to, you're the only one I can trust. Do you still have a cabin up on top of that mountain of yours?"

The stiff muscles in his back protested when he whipped his head around to glare at Sam. "Yeah, but..."

"Perfect," Sam interrupted as if it was already a done deal. He steered the car into the parking lot in front of the federal building. "I've already talked to the top dog in the Denver office and he's agreed to go along with you hiding our witness until I figure out who in the office is in cahoots with Crowley."

Sean could tell that he'd lost the battle before it ever got started. He couldn't say no to Sam's request, even though being put on guard duty was the last thing he'd anticipated when he'd been awakened in the middle of the night. He'd anticipated helping to track down a killer, not protecting a federal witness with pretty, emerald-green eyes and long, silky copper-colored hair.

It felt like the bottom dropped out of his stomach and he swallowed hard. There was no room for that train of thought in a situation like this. It was going to be his responsibility to keep her safe, and that was going to take all of his concentration as long as Crowley was in the wind. Bailey was an innocent party in this tug-of-war between the criminal and law enforcement and Sean had basically given her his word she would be protected from the fallout of that war. If stepping up to guard her personally was the only way to guarantee her safety, then that was what he'd do. He wasn't about to leave her to deal with this mess on her own, no matter how attractive he thought she was.

* * *

Bailey caught her lower lip between her teeth to keep it from quivering as she sat in an office at the federal building, waiting for Agent Fowler to explain why she'd been summoned by the FBI in the middle of the night. She glanced at the two expressionless men standing by the door. Beyond announcing that they were going to escort her to the federal building and telling her to pack a bag for several days, they hadn't spoken another word. As she continued to stare at them, their demeanor and black suits reminded her of the agents from the *Men in Black* movies. The only thing missing were the dark sunglasses. Maybe it was her nerves getting the better of her after the terrifying events of the day, but she was barely able to suppress the giggles of hysteria bubbling up inside her. She'd never in her life been under this kind of stress, nor had she ever been this afraid for this long, and she wasn't sure how much more she could endure.

The door between her two guards suddenly opened and Sean Hanson walked in, followed closely by Agent Fowler. As relieved as she was to see Sean again, his somber expression gave her reason to believe something was terribly wrong.

"Thank you for bringing Ms. O'Keefe in for us. I think we can handle things from here, gentlemen," Agent Fowler said, dismissing her impassive security detail.

When Sean settled into the chair next to hers, she looked from him to Agent Fowler seating himself behind the desk. Fowler's expression was just as grim as Sean's.

She knew she should wait to hear what he had to say, but her tension and anxiety were bubbling over and she couldn't hold back her questions any longer. "Why did you send for me in the middle of the night? Did I do something wrong? Am I in trouble for some reason? Please tell me what this is…"

"It's going to be okay, Bailey," Sean said, reaching over to take her hand in his. His reassuring touch and calming baritone cut through her panic like nothing else. Stopping her litany of questions, she took a breath and waited for him to explain further. "I'm sorry that there wasn't enough time for anyone to let you know what's happened. The first priority was to get you to safety." He took a deep breath before locking his gaze with hers. "Earlier tonight, Harold Crowley, the man who held you hostage, overpowered both of the marshals transporting him to a detention center in Denver. He's escaped federal custody and his current whereabouts are unknown."

Sean had just recited in perfect detail her worst nightmare. Only this wasn't a bad dream. It was very real. The man who threatened her life as well as Sean's was out there somewhere in the dark, free to carry out his threats. And she wasn't naïve enough to think he wouldn't. A mixture of fear and panic snaked up her spine, making her want to run and hide somewhere, anywhere, away from this chilling reality.

"We've come up with a plan to keep you safe while we find Crowley and take him back into custody," Agent Fowler assured her as if that was supposed to make her feel better about the entire situation.

"I was supposed to be safe in my own home," she pointed out, her voice trembling with emotion. She felt as if she was trapped in a really bad B movie and had no choice but to let the events play out.

"We know we dropped the ball, and you have every right to feel that we let you down." Sean was focusing all of his attention on her and it caused her stomach to feel like it had been filled with butterflies. "But Agent Fowler and I have talked it over and I'll be in charge of your safety until Crowley is caught. I give you my word that I'll do everything in my power to make sure nothing happens to you."

"Beyond you being in charge…what is this plan?" she asked. The more she learned about this Crowley person and his heinous threats, the more frightened she became. But the truth was, she did trust Sean to ensure she made it to testify at the trial. He seemed to be just as invested as she was in putting that horrible man behind bars for as long as the law allowed.

"I'm going to take you home with me and at first light, I'll get my brother to drive us up to a trailhead on Cougar Mountain. From there we'll hike up to my cabin close to the peak." He smiled. "It's off the grid and you'll be safe there. I promise."

"We're going hiking," she repeated. The closest her mother had ever allowed her to get to hiking was to walk the four blocks from their house to the library to check out books. "But there's a lot of snow in the mountains, isn't there? Why can't we use a snowmobile or some other form of transportation?"

"It would draw too much attention to us and potentially give our location away." He gave her hand an encouraging squeeze. "The fewer people who know we're up there, the better."

She knew what he said made sense, but she was thoroughly exhausted and completely overwhelmed. The past eighteen hours had been more terrifying than any she could ever remember experiencing. But the one person who had calmed her nerves, bolstered her courage and offered his life to save hers without so much as a moment's hesitation was asking her to trust him once again.

With a short nod of acceptance, she met Sean's steady gaze head-on. "When do we leave?"

THREE

"I have a case at the cabin to turn my cell phone into a satellite phone," Sean told his brother. "I'll call you to pick us up after I hear from Sam that they have Crowley in custody. Otherwise, I won't be in touch unless there's an emergency."

Blane nodded. "Dropping off the grid until they catch this lowlife is definitely in your best interest. How long do you think it will take?"

"There's no way of knowing." Sean shook his head. "If I had to guess, I'd say it won't take long. The Bureau will pull out all the stops to find him."

"Yeah, and if he shows up trying to cause trouble on Cougar Mountain, you have three brothers who'll be all over that." The man's laughter held little humor. "Mess with one of us, you get all of us and by the time we turn him over to the feds, he'll wish he'd kept on going."

Listening from the backseat of the truck, Bailey couldn't believe all of the things that had happened to her in a little less than twenty-two hours, and all because of an evil man named Harold Crowley. She'd been held at gunpoint, her life had been threatened, she'd been awakened in the middle of the night by the Men in Black of the Wyoming Highway Patrol, been whisked away to Sean's ranch—in a helicopter no less—and now, at the crack of dawn, she was sitting in a ranch truck, riding up a mountain road, to take a five-mile hike through snow above her knees in order to reach a cabin at the top of a mountain. Unbelievable! In less than a day, she had experienced more chaos and drama in her life than she ever had before. And if her mother had lived to hear about it, she would have been beyond horrified by everything that had happened.

The only child of two older parents, Bailey had a fairly normal childhood. But everything changed shortly after her twelfth birthday when her father suddenly passed away from an undetected congenital heart defect. That was when Marlene O'Keefe had become obsessive about Bailey's health and well-being. And even though the doctors had assured her that her daughter was healthy and there were no congenital defects of any kind to worry about, her mother became overly protective to the point of attempting to control every aspect of Bailey's life.

Looking back as an adult, with an adult's perspective, she could see that the protectiveness had come from love. But as a child, she hadn't had much patience with it. Her lower lip trembled from the guilt as she remembered how much she'd resented not being allowed to do all the things the other girls at school had done. She'd never been allowed to participate in sports because her mother had been afraid she'd get hurt. Even something as simple as a class field trip was out of the question unless her mother could get off work to go along as a chaperone. When it came time for her to get her driver's license, the only reason her mother had finally given in was because Bailey had agreed to attend classes at the local community college instead of leaving home to live in a dorm at one of the state universities. Her mother's controlling tendencies had been extreme, but Bailey knew her mother had been terrified she'd lose her only child, the child she'd prayed so hard and so long for the Lord to let her have.

And just look at her now. After a lifetime of playing it safe, of not taking any chances, she'd still ended up here, with a killer on her trail.

She took several deep breaths to keep her emotions under control. After the events of yesterday and the trials she knew she'd face today and every day until Crowley was caught, she could almost see her mother's reasoning in wanting to avoid any potential danger. Too bad it hadn't worked.

"It's supposed to start snowing around noon, so my tire tracks won't be an issue for too much longer." Blane's statement drew her back to the present and the brothers' conversation. "Be sure you're off the trail and settled in the cabin as soon as possible. It's supposed to be blizzard conditions by midafternoon."

"Thanks for the weather update. I didn't have time to check the forecast before we left." Sean pulled a warm-looking knitted beanie from his coat pocket and handed it to her. "We'll reach our drop-off point in about five minutes. Put this on. It'll help keep you warm for the hike up to the cabin."

"Thank you." She pulled the beanie on

and tightened the scarf she'd crocheted last winter around her neck. She looked down at the knee-high snow boots Blane had borrowed for her from his ranch foreman's wife. "And Blane, please thank your foreman's wife for loaning me these boots and mittens."

"I'm more than happy to help," Blane answered. She'd overheard him tell Sean while she was putting on the boots that when he asked to borrow them, the man hadn't questioned why he needed them and Blane hadn't told the man.

"All this snow is going to take some getting used to. Where I'm from—in the very southernmost part of Illinois—snowfalls are usually only an inch or two deep, when they happened at all."

"The elevation in Eagle Fork isn't as high as in the mountains and it doesn't usually start getting a lot of snow until mid-to-late December," Sean said, pulling on a knit hat like the one he'd given her. "It won't take long for you to acclimate to Wyoming weather."

"How long have you been in Wyoming, Bailey?" Blane asked conversationally as he steered the truck through a hairpin turn on a snow-packed road like it was no big deal.

"It will be two months next week," she answered without looking up. She didn't want to see how close the truck was to the edge of the impossibly narrow, winding road.

"So this will be your first time in Eagle Fork during the Christmas Jubilee." Blane laughed. "Believe me, you're going to love it. It's always the weekend before Christmas and the entire town shows up."

"Don't mind my brother," Sean said, grinning at her over his shoulder. "The only person I know of who gets more excited by the holidays than a little kid is Blane."

"I can't help it. It's my favorite holiday," Blane said, good-naturedly. He parked the truck on a wider stretch of the road and turned to look at Bailey in the backseat. "It was nice meeting you, Bailey. I just wish it had been under better circumstances."

"I wish so, too, Blane. Thanks again for your help."

Sean got out of the truck and then stepped over to lift her down from the backseat. It seemed like an intimate gesture, but considering how high the truck was, it was more out of necessity than anything else. If he hadn't helped her, she might've done a face plant in the snow and shown the Hanson brothers just how truly graceless she could be.

"Th-thank you." Why did being this close to Sean always make her feel so flustered? "Is…this the…trailhead?"

"No, we'll walk through the trees from here to the trail. I didn't want the snow at the trailhead to show any signs of human activity." Sean pulled the backpack with their things from the seat and winced as he shrugged it onto his back. "I'll be in touch when I get the all-clear," he told Blane as he removed a rifle from the gun rack in the back window.

Blane nodded. "You two take care and I'll see you in a few days."

As soon as Sean closed the door, Blane put the dual-wheeled truck in gear. The powerful diesel engine rumbled as he turned the truck around and headed back down the mountain.

Bailey stared as it disappeared from sight. Even though she'd only gotten a brief glimpse of it, she envied the relationship she'd observed between the two brothers. She'd always been convinced that a person couldn't really miss what they'd never had. But now? Seeing firsthand the closeness between the men, the bond of love and caring they shared, made her sad that she hadn't had that in her life.

"Ready?" Sean asked.

"I suppose I'm as ready as I'll ever be," she said, forcing a smile. As long as she could remember she'd wanted new experiences and exciting adventures in her life. She just hadn't expected them to come with a good-looking man and a hazard warning.

"Let's stop to rest," Sean said when he noticed Bailey was even farther behind than she had been earlier. They were making good time and only had another mile to go, so they could afford a break—as long as they kept it short. The storm front was moving in and he wanted them to make it before the snow started falling.

"I just thought of something." She leaned back against the trunk of a huge lodgepole pine tree. "Wouldn't it have been easier if we'd used snowshoes for this hike?"

He nodded. "Yes. But unfortunately, we didn't have time for you to get used to walking in them. You said this morning at the FBI office you're not a hiker, so I'm guessing you haven't used snowshoes before?" She shook her head, and he continued. "You learning to walk in them might have been easier on your legs but it would have slowed us down even more." He gave her what he hoped was an encouraging smile. "We only have another mile to go. We'll be there in another thirty to forty-five minutes. Tops."

"Was it really only this morning that we were at the FBI office?" She groaned. "It feels like it was at least a week ago."

He nodded. "Did you get any sleep at all before the state troopers brought you into the office?" As nerve-racking as her day had been, he'd be surprised if she'd been able to get any rest at all.

"No." She brushed a strand of her long, silky hair from her cheek. "Every time I closed my eyes I could see that horrible man sneering at me while he pointed his gun between my eyes. And if that wasn't bad enough, every sound in the house I'm renting made me think he was trying to get inside or had already broken in and was coming after me."

Sean had never wanted to break someone's face as much as he did Harold Crowley's. Any man who traumatized a woman should be treated to a dose of his own medicine and Sean would be more than happy to be the one dispensing the cure to Crowley.

"After we get to the cabin and eat lunch, you can take a nap while I get everything up and running." He checked his watch. "If you feel rested enough, we should get going."

"Lead the way," she said, shoving away from the tree.

Behind her smile he could see the toll the past twenty-four hours had taken on her. But to her credit, he hadn't heard one complaint out of her. In the short time he'd known her, he'd discovered that Bailey had the courage and strength to handle whatever came her way and made the best of it. He admired that.

Forty minutes later, just as the first snowflakes started floating down, they came to the clearing. There his cabin sat, nestled against the timberline of lodgepole pines and blue spruce trees. Everything looked as it should and there weren't any tracks near the log buildings, other than a few rabbit, fox and deer trails.

"This is your cabin?" Bailey looked around. "It almost looks like a smaller version of that beautiful log ranch house of yours." She gave him a puzzled glance. "You led me to believe it was a lot more rustic than this."

"I didn't say *rustic*, exactly. What I said was it's off the grid." Shaking his head, he grinned and put his gloved hand to the small of her back as he guided her up the steps and across the porch to the front door. "That doesn't have to mean we'll be roughing it."

After unlocking the padlock, he opened the solid wood door and quickly glanced around to make sure nothing had been disturbed since his last visit. Only a handful of people even knew about the place and he really hadn't anticipated any problems. But he hadn't expected Crowley to escape custody, either. It was the unanticipated situations that caused Sean to adopt the motto that an abundance of caution was never a bad idea.

"Stay here by the door while I do a quick sweep of the cabin," he said, closing and locking the door behind them. He removed his gloves and held the rifle at the ready as he moved methodically from room to room, clearing them in military fashion and searching for any sign that something wasn't the way he'd left it. By the time he cleared both floors he was satisfied there wasn't anything out of place and nothing to worry about. "All clear."

There was no response.

"Bailey?" he called a little louder.

When she failed to answer, his mind went to the worst-case scenario and he rushed downstairs. He found her completely engrossed in the pictures he'd taken of the wildlife on the mountain.

"These are beautiful. Did you take them?" she asked when he stopped beside her.

He released the breath he hadn't realized he'd been holding and engaging the safety, placed his rifle on the gun rack above the fireplace mantel. "Yeah, I did. Photography's something I got into a few years ago after I resigned from the FBI." He hoped she wouldn't dig deeper into his explanation. He didn't want to get into his reasons for resigning or how getting into photography had helped him come to terms with the failure and guilt he'd had after losing a hostage. It would not only shake her confidence in his ability to protect her, it would also dredge up a past he'd worked hard to distance himself from.

"Did you make these, as well?" she asked, touching one of the rough-hewn frames. "They look old and rugged. They're perfect for pictures of wildlife."

"Thanks, but I really can't take a whole lot of credit." Since she seemed totally preoccupied by the pictures, he decided to go ahead and begin implementing his security measures while they talked. He opened the backpack to remove the case with his service sidearm and several loaded clips of ammunition. "I helped Blane clean up the remnants of a hundred-and-fifty-year-old tool shed that collapsed during a thunderstorm." He laughed as he placed the gun case on the mantel. "Believe me, the lumber looked pretty rugged after that. All I did was pick up some of it for small projects and then cut and nailed a few of the boards together."

"Well, I think you did a beautiful job of making the frames, as well as taking the pictures." She removed her coat, hat and scarf to hang on one of the pegs beside the door. "I admire creativity because I'm so bad at it myself. About the only thing I can do besides crochet is cook."

"Hey, don't sell yourself short." Turning to face her, he grinned. "Take it from a man who appreciates a good meal. Cooking is important. And just for the record, crocheting and knitting are skills that shouldn't be downplayed. My Grandma Jean knitted the hats we wore today and she'd take a strip off my hide if I didn't defend the skill required for the needle arts."

"I think I like your grandmother. A lot." Bailey's light laughter caused a warmth in his chest that he wasn't ready to deal with.

Needing to put a little distance between them to get things back into perspective, he walked over to the door. "I'm going to go… check the solar storage batteries to make sure we have plenty of electricity. Make yourself at home. I'll only be a few minutes."

When he returned to the cabin several minutes later, Sean had his resolve to keep things strictly business between himself and Bailey firmly in place. Once it was safe for her to return to her life in Eagle Fork, she'd go back to working at the bank and doing whatever else she did and he'd return to his ranch to tend his cattle and take pictures of the animals on top of his mountain. Their lives would never intersect again. And that was the way things were meant to be.

When he hung his coat up and pulled off his boots, he turned to find Bailey curled up on the leather couch, sound asleep. Crossing the hardwood floor, he took the throw draped over the back of the armchair and covered her with it. Her silky copper hair framed her pretty face and complemented her peaches-and-cream complexion. His breath lodged in his lungs. She was absolutely beautiful and unless he missed his guess, she wasn't even aware of it.

He sighed heavily. There was a time when he had thought he'd like to find someone like her to settle down with, raise a few kids, then spend their golden years together sitting in rocking chairs on the porch, reminiscing about decades of love and happiness. But so many years of dealing with the ugly side of society had left its share of marks on him and he knew he couldn't expose a woman, and especially one he loved, to that kind of baggage.

Forcing himself to walk away and forget about the longing that sometimes kept him awake at night, he crossed to the door on the other side of the kitchen to the cabin's control room. He needed to check the settings on the alarm system and make sure they had a "go bag" ready in case they needed to make a fast and unexpected getaway.

When Bailey woke up, she experienced a moment of panic as she looked around the dimly lit cabin and tried to remember where she was. Her heart rate began to steady when her memories of the events of the past day and a half returned. She was in Sean's cabin and the last thing she remembered was lying down on the couch to rest her tired muscles from their hike in the snow while Sean checked on something in a shed outside.

"Are you ready for supper?" Sean asked quietly from the armchair at the end of the couch.

She pushed her hair back from her face and noticed that the curtains were all pulled. "How long have I been asleep?"

"Close to four hours." He put the book he'd been reading on the end table. "If you're hungry, I'll put the biscuits in the oven and dish up the stew."

"I know it isn't very ladylike to admit it, but I'm absolutely starved." She looked around to see if there was an obvious place to freshen up.

As if reading her mind, he pointed toward a door on the opposite side of the room. "The downstairs bathroom is the door to the left of the stairs."

"Is there a shower?" she asked hopefully when she noticed his thick, dark hair was damp and he had on fresh clothes. The idea of showering sounded amazing.

"Sure." He smiled. "There are towels in the cabinet, along with soap and shampoo. I'm not sure about an extra toothbrush. Sorry."

"I've got that covered. Somewhere in that big backpack, I have a travel case with everything I need." She hesitated. She'd always been taught not to go through other people's things without their permission. "Do you mind if I rummage through the pack to find it?"

"Go right ahead." He turned to put a pan in the oven. "Supper will be ready in about twenty minutes."

Exactly twenty minutes later Bailey emerged from the bathroom feeling refreshed and thoroughly impressed by the details Sean had put into his "off the grid" cabin. "This is really amazing," she said as she put her laundry bag and travel case in the backpack. "There's hot and cold running water, electricity, a fully functioning kitchen and central heat. Is there anything you didn't think of?"

Smiling, he set two glasses of milk on the table beside steaming bowls of the most delicious-smelling stew. "Well, besides a fully stocked pantry and freezer, the running water, electricity and alarm system, I made sure that everything is either composted or goes through a treatment and filtration system to keep things environmentally friendly and safe for animals—both of the two-legged and four-legged varieties."

"That's wonderful." She joined him at the table. When she bowed her head to bless the meal, Sean startled her when he took her hand in his and bowed his head, as well, gesturing for her to speak. "Thank You for this day, dear Lord, and thank You for this food we are about to eat. Please watch over us throughout the night and keep us safe from harm. Amen."

"Amen," Sean repeated, and squeezed her hand. She cleared her suddenly dry throat and did her best to ignore her reaction to him. To distract herself, she tried to focus on what he'd said about the cabin. "I know you wanted all of the conveniences here that you have at your ranch, but I'm not sure I understand the need for such an extensive alarm system. Why would you need that if only a few people know your cabin is up here?"

"I installed it to let me know what animals are prowling around here at night. If a bear tries to break into the cabin while I'm gone, the loud noise from the house alarm will hopefully scare them away." He passed her a plate of biscuits that smelled absolutely wonderful. "I hadn't planned to use this place as a safe house, but I'm glad for all the safety precautions now. The alarm system is adding an extra layer of security to help me keep you safe while we wait for Sam to let us know it's clear to return to Eagle Fork." He pointed to the drawn curtains. "I installed blackout curtains on all the windows so animals will avoid getting close to the cabin at night." Nodding toward the wall with the pictures he'd taken, he smiled. "That photo of the bobcat was taken last winter when he decided to pay me a midnight visit. He wouldn't have come that close if he'd been able to see the lights. It's a bonus now that the curtains are preventing anyone from detecting we're here."

"Just one more layer of security," she said, smiling as she repeated his earlier comment.

They ate in companionable silence for several long moments when a sudden beeping sound invaded the quiet. "What on earth is that?" she asked, looking around to see where the noise was coming from.

"The perimeter alarms. It's probably a deer or a bobcat." But Sean immediately jumped to his feet to enter a room off the kitchen. Reappearing only a few seconds later, he pointed toward their coats by the door as he headed for the fireplace. "Get your boots and coat on." His voice was barely above a whisper, his tone tense as he reached for the rifle above the mantel. "We have to leave. Now!"

FOUR

While Bailey hurriedly pulled on her boots and coat, Sean did the same. By his estimation, they had less than five minutes before the cabin was breached and with the open floorplan downstairs, they would become sitting ducks. He'd thought about standing their ground in one of the upstairs bedrooms, but with their only exits on the first floor—short of jumping out a window, which he'd rather avoid—he couldn't take the chance of being trapped with no way out, especially since he had two armed assailants to deal with.

Grabbing the go bag he'd readied earlier, he slung it over his shoulder, grabbed his rifle and quickly ushered Bailey toward the control room. The lights suddenly went out and he knew whoever was out there had cut the power off at the shed storing the solar batteries. It would take the assailants roughly two minutes to make it from the shed to the house and a few seconds more to shoot the lock off the front door.

He quickly released the Maglite he'd clipped to the pack, pulled back part of the carpet under the desk and shined the beam on the metal trap door. "We're going to have to take the secret route out of here," he said, lifting the steel panel to shine the light on the ladder leading down into the tunnel beneath the cabin. When she leaned over and looked into the dark hole, then looked back at him, he could tell she wasn't wild about the idea of going down into what looked like a bottomless pit. But it was their only hope of making a quick getaway without being spotted by Crowley and whoever else was out there with him. "I promise I'll be right behind you."

She seemed to understand the urgency, even though he'd been vague about the situation. Telling her that he'd spotted two intruders could wait until they reached safety. The last thing he wanted to do was cause her more stress than she was already under or worse yet, cause her to panic.

Bailey looked at him a split second longer as if making a decision before she nodded, took a deep breath and began to descend the ladder. As soon as he heard her boots touch the concrete floor below, he climbed halfway down the aluminum rungs, reached up to make sure the carpet would settle back in place over the door when he closed it, then pulled it shut. After securing the dead bolt, he dropped down onto the tunnel floor and, stepping around Bailey, motioned for her to follow.

"He'll probably find the door, but it should keep him busy for a while trying to get it open." Sean shined the light into the long corridor as they started the uphill walk to the exit. "By then, we'll be safely hidden on the other side of the mountain."

"But what if he picks the lock?" she asked. "Isn't part of being a robber knowing how to do that?"

"Not going to happen." He grinned at her over his shoulder. "It's a single-sided dead bolt and can only be unlocked from this side of the door."

She nodded. "In other words, even if he could pick a lock, there's nothing on the other side to pick?"

"Yup."

He couldn't help but grin when he heard her murmur, "Just another layer of security."

They walked along the tunnel at a fast

pace for several minutes and Sean felt guilty for pushing Bailey so hard. He knew she was tired and while he was glad she'd had time for a nap, a shower and part of a hot meal, he knew that wasn't nearly enough to make up for the sleep she'd lost or the emotional toll that being held at gunpoint had to have taken on her. But they didn't have a choice. They needed to put as much distance between themselves and the cabin as possible.

Sean stopped several minutes later when he felt cold air snaking its way down toward them from the opening up close to the peak of the mountain. "We're getting close to the end of the tunnel. Did you bring the hat I gave you and your mittens?"

"Right here." She removed the hat from her coat pocket and pulled it on, then did the same with the mittens.

He tugged his own hat down over his ears. "Better get ready for a blast of cold air."

He hated that Bailey was going to get the full force of the cold December wind as soon as they exited the tunnel. But Old Man Winter always flexed his muscles a little earlier in the mountains than other places, and the jet stream, combined with the altitude, made the wind blow just about all the time in this part of the state. They'd be coming out just a couple of hundred feet or so from the mountaintop and that meant they were going to be buffeted with gusts that were, at times, gale force.

He waited until she wrapped her scarf around her neck and covered her mouth and nose before he unlocked and pulled open the barred gate he had installed to keep animals from using the stone corridor as a den for the winter. "Stay directly behind me and I'll block most of the wind off of you," he said, relocking the gate. "And it wouldn't be a bad idea for you to hold on to the back of my coat until we get to the other side of the peak. That will keep us from being separated, as well as helping you stay on your feet if you get hit by a big gust of wind."

"Okay." Her luminous emerald eyes were wide with apprehension, but as usual, she didn't argue. Instead, she took hold of his coat and followed him out of the tunnel.

His admiration for her courageous and uncomplaining nature went up another notch. She hadn't shown so much as a trace of hesitation when they stepped out into the cold, snowy night to hike over the mountaintop. Fortunately, Sean knew the mountain like the back of his hand and even on a moonless night he knew within inches where every deer trail, mountain goat path and bobcat route were located. But Bailey didn't know any of that and he felt honored by her obvious trust in him to lead her to safety.

He knew her confidence in him would likely disappear faster than a June frost once she found out where they would be holing up for the rest of the night. The cave on the other side of the mountain where they were going to take shelter wasn't far, but it was nothing like one of the warm, comfortable bedrooms they'd left back at his cabin. After all she'd been through, he felt like a jerk for making her hike uphill in the snow again, all so they could sleep in a cave hidden by a grouping of boulders. But their options were limited and they needed a place to hide out from Crowley and whoever was helping him, as well as a place where he could plan out their next move.

By the time Sean stopped at a narrow opening between two boulders, Bailey's leg muscles felt like limp noodles from wading through the deep snow. Not to mention, she didn't think she'd ever been as cold in her entire life as she was just then. The wind had been fierce, the clouds blocked out any light from the moon and stars and the swirling snow had been so disorienting, she didn't know how Sean had been able to keep them from walking right off the side of the peak.

He'd tried to say something to her, but the howling wind ripped it away and she had no idea what he wanted her to do. That was when he shrugged out of the backpack, took her hand in his, turned sideways and urged her to do the same as they inched their way through the tight opening between the boulders to enter a small cave.

It was a physical relief not to feel the pressure of the wind pushing at her. Even the sound of the wind was considerably quieter inside the small space as he dropped the backpack by the back wall and shined his flashlight over the cave's interior. "I'm afraid this isn't as comfortable as the cabin, but it's dry and will shelter us from the wind and snow."

She nodded as she looked around. "I-I'm impressed at…h-how hidden it is. U-unless you know it's here…y-you could walk right by it and…n-not find it." She wrapped her arms around herself in an attempt to hold in as much of her body heat as she could. Whether it was from the cold or a case of nerves—or, most likely, a combination of the two—she couldn't stop shivering.

Her stomach did a funny little flip when Sean moved to stand in front of her and, reaching out, began to rub his hands up and down her upper arms. Even through her coat and sweatshirt it did help to chase away a bit of the chill.

"I'm sorry I can't build a fire, but I don't want to run the risk of the smoke giving away our location or having the wind drive it back inside the cave."

"Th-that wouldn't be...g-good." She tried to sound as unconcerned as her chattering teeth would allow. "Sm-smoke inhalation is...n-never advisable."

His low chuckle sent a shiver through her that had nothing whatsoever to do with the cold or her jangled nerves. What on earth was wrong with her? They were running for their lives and she was close to becoming an ice sculpture. Shouldn't she be focusing more on the gravity of their situation and less on how wonderful his strong hands felt as he tried to help her warm up?

When Sean stepped away to pick up the backpack, the chill returned. She did her best to ignore it.

"We're going to have to get you warm."

He dug around in the backpack until he found a small, folded flannel blanket along with a nylon bag with some kind of thin material that looked a lot like aluminum foil. "This won't be nearly as toasty as the cabin would have been, but it will keep us from freezing."

"That's one of those space blankets, isn't it?" She knew it was supposed to retain the heat generated by a person's own body to help them stay warm, but it didn't seem possible that something that looked that flimsy would be able to do much.

He nodded as he spread the flannel blanket on the stone floor and sat down with his back against the wall. "Sit beside me," he said, beckoning her to join him. When she sat down, he opened the lapels of his coat. "Open your coat, then settle against my chest and we'll share our body heat to warm up."

At the moment she was so cold she would cozy up to a hibernating grizzly bear if she thought it would help her get warm. When she settled against his broad chest, he pulled his coat as close together as it would go around them. Then he tugged the thin silver cover over them before he turned out the flashlight.

"I know this is going to sound like a dumb question, considering we're sitting in the dark, on the stone floor of a cave, in sub-freezing weather, but are you comfortable?" His voice sounded apologetic.

"S-surprisingly… I am," she answered, already feeling a bit warmer. Her teeth had slowed down to an occasional chatter and with the side of her head resting on his broad chest, the strong, steady beat of his heart was a calming reassurance to her rattled nerves.

"Good. I can't have you turning into a Popsicle on my watch."

His low voice, the voice that had gotten her through all the horrible events of the past two days, soothed her once again and she began to relax. They sat in silence for several minutes before she spoke again. "Do you mind if I ask you a question?"

"Not at all. What do you want to know?"

"What's it like to have three siblings?" She hoped it wasn't too personal, but Blane had mentioned Sean having three brothers and she couldn't help wondering how different her life would have been if she'd had more family.

"Well, it was pretty crazy when we were all younger." His quiet laugh made her smile and she could picture in her mind the fond expression on his handsome face. "The four of us are pretty close in age and believe me, there was never a dull moment when we were growing up."

"Your poor mother," Bailey said, wondering how the woman survived.

"Yeah, she definitely had her hands full."

"Who's the oldest?"

"Me. I'm thirty-five, Levi is thirty-four, then Blane is after him at thirty-two and at thirty-one, Thad is the baby of the Hanson brothers. Or as we used to call ourselves when we were kids, the Cougar Mountain Mavericks."

"Mavericks?"

He laughed. "Yeah. Wild, unpredictable and generally all but impossible to keep track of or to control."

"Do you have sisters?"

"No. I think my mom decided that four boys were about all she could handle."

Bailey could hear the love in his voice when Sean talked about his family and she was reminded again just how alone she was. With no close relatives left and only a handful of distant cousins she had never met, she really had no shared history. There was no one she could reminisce with about child-hood memories; no one who had the same connection to her family.

"What about you?" he asked. "Do you have brothers and sisters?"

She shook her head. "No. I think my parents would have loved having more children, but they had tried to have a child for years and were in their midforties when they finally had me. Apparently, it was a pretty tough pregnancy and after I was born, the doctor advised them that it would be unwise to try having more children."

"Do your folks still live in Illinois?"

"No." Bailey wasn't sure she wanted to tell him that she was totally alone in the world. Also, she didn't like having anyone feeling sorry for her and especially not Sean.

His arms tightened around her. "Do your parents know what's happened over the past couple of days?"

She shrugged one shoulder, choosing to remain silent. What could she say that wouldn't make her sound sad and pathetic?

Sean remained quiet for several long moments before he leaned his head down to whisper in her ear. "Try not to make any noise. We've got company just outside the cave entrance."

* * *

Sean felt Bailey's slight body tense against him as he listened to two different voices close to the crack between the boulders. He couldn't tell what they were saying due to the wind and the muffled hush that always accompanied falling snow, but he got the impression they were arguing about something. Reaching for his sidearm in the holster on his belt, he released the safety. "Just sit real still and say a little prayer that they don't notice the crevice between the rocks," he whispered. The only outward signs that she'd heard him were the almost imperceptible nod of her head and the tightening of the fistful of his shirt she clutched in her hand.

He knew the men wouldn't find his and Bailey's tracks. The wind and blowing snow had erased those almost immediately and there wouldn't be any trace of them taking shelter in the cave. But if Crowley and his cohort got curious about the narrow space between the boulders...well, that was a different story. He'd been forced to shoot several men in the line of duty when he was working for the Bureau, though fortunately, he'd never before had to take a life. But that didn't mean he wouldn't or that he'd think twice about taking that shot if it came down to a matter of life or death for Bailey. He had accepted the assignment of keeping her safe and that was exactly what he intended to do.

There must have been a lull in the gusts of wind because he distinctly heard a gravelly voice he knew had to be Crowley's. "You go right ahead and see where that crack leads if you want to, but I'm not going to waste my time dragging what's left of your sorry carcass out of there if you stir up a bear or a mountain lion."

Bracing himself to take immediate action if necessary, Sean waited to see if whoever was with Crowley had the courage to squeeze through the narrow opening. But no one entered and it suddenly grew quiet outside except for the howls of the gusting wind. Not daring to move, Sean waited a good ten or fifteen minutes before he finally relaxed, reengaged the safety on his gun and replaced it back into the leather holster on his belt.

"I'd say they've decided to move on." When she didn't respond, he started to become concerned. "Bailey?"

She murmured his name but didn't move.

"Are you okay?" he asked, realizing that

at some point she'd grasped the front of his shirt with both of her fists.

When she answered he wasn't certain, but he thought he heard her say something about being a victim. "Bailey, everything is going to be all right." He turned on the flashlight to let her see the determination in his expression. "I give you my word that I'm not going to let anything happen to you."

Releasing his shirt, she raised her head from his chest and looked him square in the eyes. The determination in her green gaze was amazing, as well as a complete surprise to him. "I know you'll do everything you can to keep me safe, Sean. And you have no idea how much that means to me. But I'm not going to let this horrible man make me feel like a victim. He's not going to get the better of me or my nerves, no matter how many times he shoves a gun in my face or makes us take off running to get away from him. I refuse to give him that kind of power over me."

Sean couldn't help but grin. He'd never met a woman quite like her. She was barely taller than five feet and a smile, and she'd be lucky if she weighed a buck and a nickel soaking wet. But she was full of life and had more spirit and courage in her little finger than a lot of men he had met. A man would be smart to hang on to a woman like Bailey and never let her go.

His heart came to a screeching halt and his grin faded. He needed to remember that finding a woman to have and to hold wasn't in his future, no matter how amazing she might be. He was only with Bailey to keep her alive and see that she was available to testify and put a career criminal behind bars for the rest of his miserable life.

"There's no way anyone would ever think of you as a victim, Bailey. You're one of the strongest people I've ever met."

"Thank you—" she covered a yawn with her hand "—Sean. I've never thought of myself that way."

He shifted to a more comfortable position and tightened his arms around her. He told himself it was to share more of his warmth with her, but the truth was she felt good in his arms. It was something he wasn't entirely comfortable thinking about, but he could brush it aside if he reminded himself that it was helping her. Besides, he was sure she wouldn't read anything into it. Surely, she wasn't in the market for a tired, old exfederal agent.

"We might as well get some sleep. I don't

think Crowley and whoever he has with him will bother us again tonight."

"Wait." She sat up to stare at him. "You mean there's more than one man out there trying to kill us?"

Busted! He'd meant to tell her once they reached the cave, but she'd been tired and on the verge of hypothermia. His first priority had been to get her warmed up, then Crowley and his cohort had shown up. She'd only just calmed down in the aftermath of that.

"Yes. I noticed it on the surveillance camera when we had to leave the cabin. I thought you might have heard the two voices..."

"I didn't pay attention. I was too busy praying whoever was out there wouldn't venture into the cave. But that's beside the point. You didn't think it was important enough to tell me there were two of them when we left the cabin?"

"I didn't want to scare you." All things considered, his reasoning did sound pretty lame. The woman had stared down the barrel of a gun without losing her nerve and had fled for her life over the boulder-strewn top of a mountain in the dark. What was the difference in knowing there were two men chasing them instead of just one?

"From now on don't worry about me

being frightened." She shook her head as she yawned again. "Let me assure you, my days of being a hothouse flower are over with for good."

He stared at her for a moment as he tried to figure out what she meant. Deciding it could wait, he met her emerald gaze head-on. "I swear to you that from now on I'll be completely transparent about what's going on."

"Good." She laid her head against his chest. "I'm finding it hard...to keep my eyes..."

He smiled and turned off the flashlight. She'd fallen asleep in midsentence. He would have liked to think the reason she'd gone to sleep so quickly was because he'd made her feel safe. But the truth was, it had probably been less a question of nodding off and more her passing out from being thoroughly exhausted.

He frowned and leaned his head back against the wall of the cave. What was wrong with him? In the span of ten minutes he'd thought about making Bailey his and never letting her go, as well as wanting to be her hero.

Maybe Bailey wasn't the only one suffering from exhaustion. Yeah, that had to be it.

All he needed was a good night's sleep to clear his mind and get himself back on track. And if he believed that, mules could fly.

FIVE

When Bailey opened her eyes, she was lying on the floor of the cave with her head resting on Sean's backpack and the space blanket tucked in around her. Turning her head, she could see a dim shaft of light filtering into the small cavern from the crack between the boulders and decided it must be morning. But where was Sean? As she lay there, thoughts of the night before and how they'd almost been discovered had her sitting up to look around the small space.

"Sean?" she whispered as loudly as she dared.

When it became apparent he wasn't within easy earshot, she tried to think what could have caused him to leave. Had he heard something and left to check it out? Or had he been lured out of the cave by someone and been hurt?

His exit must not have been hurried because he'd taken the time to retrieve the backpack from the other side of the cave to use as a pillow for her.

As she sat there wondering where he went and what she should do if he failed to return, the small shaft of light was suddenly blocked by something and she held her breath as she waited to see who or what was entering the cave. Glancing around, she couldn't find anything to use to protect herself. She thought about rummaging through the backpack for some kind of weapon, but it was too late for that now. The dark silhouette of a man had just emerged from the cave entrance and to her immense relief, when he turned on his flashlight it was Sean.

His expression turned sheepish when he saw that she was awake. "Sorry I wasn't here when you woke up, but I had to go a little farther than I planned to get a signal on the sat phone." He walked over to sit down beside her. "I got hold of Blane and he and I worked out a plan to get us off the mountain."

It looked like they would be taking another hike in the snow. Not her favorite thing to do, but neither was being chased by a bad guy and his sidekick, over the top of a mountain, in the dark, to spend the night in the luxurious Ritz Cavern.

"Okay, when do we leave?" She could tell by the look on his face that she probably wasn't going to like his answer.

"Not until tonight." He quickly held up one hand as if he expected her to protest. "I know it's not ideal, but we don't know where Crowley is. He could very well still be up here on the mountain, waiting to see if we head back to the cabin."

"So you're saying we won't be going back the way we came—the way that leads to the cabin, right?" When he nodded, she had to ask, "How *are* we going to get down the mountain?"

"We're going to go down a trail on this side of the mountain into a valley where Blane can meet us." He rubbed the back of his neck with his gloved hand as if trying to relax the muscles. "And we're going to have to travel after it gets dark."

"After dark," she repeated. "Because we would be more likely to be spotted in the daylight?"

"That's right." He took her mittened hand in his. "I wish there were some other way. But the chances of being seen are greatly reduced if we travel at night."

"It's going to take us longer to get to the bottom of the mountain and it's also going to be more dangerous in the dark, isn't it?"

He gave her hand a little squeeze as he nodded. "We won't be able to get it done in one night. It's going to take us a couple of nights to get from here to the valley and I'm not going to lie to you. It will be treacherous. But I promise you, I know this mountain as well as I know my own backyard and I'll make sure you're safe."

She shook her head. "I'm not worried about that. You've already gone above and beyond what most people would do to keep me out of harm's way."

His dark-chocolate eyes searched hers for a moment. "Then why don't you tell me what has you worried?"

Bailey felt a tiny little shiver streak up her spine as she continued to stare into Sean's intense gaze. What was there about the man that fascinated her to the point of not being able to think clearly?

"I'm not really worried so much as curious." She smiled. "Is there another cave with deluxe accommodations for two about halfway down the trail?"

"No, but I happen to be pretty good with pine boughs and space blankets under a rock overhang," he said, laughing. "And something else in our favor is the fact that it should be a few degrees warmer the closer we get to the valley."

"Oh good. A little bit of a heat wave," she said, grinning. "You won't hear me grumble if it gets warmer."

He shook his head. "I haven't heard you complain about anything except me not telling you that Crowley has somebody with him."

"What's to complain about? You're keeping me alive." She glanced up at him from beneath her lashes. "And I can't thank you enough for being so diligent about it. If you weren't, I'd probably be nothing more than a memory right now."

He shrugged. "I must not be too good at it or we'd still be in the cabin."

"About that, how did he know we were there?" she asked. "I didn't think anyone but you and Agent Fowler were supposed to know where we were going—or even that I was with you at all."

"That's a good question. I've been trying to figure that out myself." His frown was dark and formidable. "We knew there was a leak in the Cheyenne office, but I know Sam wouldn't have told anyone about our plans. There had to be someone at the field office who overheard us talking the other night before we left."

"I guess that makes sense. Are you going to get in touch with Agent Fowler to let him know about the change in plans?" She hoped he didn't. After all that had happened, the only person she trusted was Sean.

"I need to let him know that Crowley is working with someone and from all indications it's someone in the Cheyenne office, but our whereabouts will stay on a need-to-know basis." He pointed his index finger at his own chest, then at her. "And right now nobody but me, you and my brothers need to know."

"That makes me feel a little better." Something he'd said earlier caused her to ask, "Won't going down to the valley on this side of the mountain put us a lot farther away from your ranch?" She wasn't an expert on hiking mountain trails by any means, considering yesterday had been the first time she'd hiked in her life. But it seemed to her that it would take a lot longer to get back to the safety of his ranch.

He reached for the backpack and began digging around inside one of the front pockets. A minute later he pulled out a couple of protein bars. Handing her one, he shook his head as he pulled two bottles of water from a side pocket. "We're not going back to my ranch. We'll be heading to the line shack at the opposite end of the valley."

When he reached for her hand, she placed hers in his and bowed her head to pray. "Dear Lord, thank You for this new day and for this food we are about to eat. And please watch over us and keep us safe as we make our way back down the mountain. In Your name we pray. Amen."

Unwrapping the honey, oats and nut bar, she asked, "Are you sure whoever owns the place won't mind us using the shack?"

"Nope." He handed her one of the plastic bottles of water. "My family owns Cougar Mountain and most of the land around it, but we won't be staying there for any length of time. That's just the pickup point where Blane and Levi will meet us."

She chewed thoughtfully on the protein bar. "Wow. I've never known anyone who owned their own mountain."

"It's actually land that my dad's great-great-grandfather settled back in the late eighteen hundreds. It sounds impressive but as far as mountains go, it's not all that big." He took a drink from his water bottle. "My brothers and I are the sixth generation of Hanson ranchers to make it our home. We incorporated a few years back, after our dad signed the ranch over to me and my brothers. We became equal partners so that the land doesn't get split up. But we all claimed a part of the property as our own personal space. Mine is the western side of the mountain where my cabin is, along with several hundred acres including my ranch house, right at the base of the mountain."

"Who owns this part?" she asked, finishing the protein bar. She found the way the brothers had worked out ownership of the huge property quite fascinating.

"Levi got this eastern side, Blane got the south end and Thad claimed the northern part." He crushed his empty water bottle, replaced the cap and stowed it in a pocket on the backpack. "We get to work together, but not so closely that we're in each other's faces all the time."

"I really envy your relationship with your brothers," she said wistfully. She'd always longed for a big, noisy, affectionate family. While she'd never doubted her mother's love, there was no denying that her childhood had been very lonely. Her mom had been so protective that it had been hard to even have close friends. It only took turning down so many invitations to sleepovers and birthday parties and trips to the mall before the invites stopped coming. By the time she was in high school, she didn't have anyone she was close to. That meant there was no one there to defend her when others marked her as an ideal victim for bullying. The teasing and humiliation got so bad that she closed herself off even more—— while people who had been at least somewhat friendly started to avoid her entirely, not wanting to draw attention from the bullies to themselves. All of which just made her feel more isolated and alone.

"I feel very fortunate," he said, nodding.

Bailey could tell by the look on his handsome face that he had more questions about her family or, more accurately, the lack thereof. But it wasn't something she wanted to go into. Deciding it was time for a change of subject, she feigned a yawn. "If we're going to be here until nightfall, do you mind if I take a little nap?"

He paused for several long moments as he seemed to study her face before he finally nodded. "That's actually a pretty good idea," he said, putting away the wrappers from their protein bars. "We'll be leaving as soon as it gets dark this evening and hopefully make it to the halfway point a little before daylight tomorrow morning."

"I thought you told me this mountain isn't all that big," she said, straightening the flannel blanket on the stone floor.

"It's not, but we'll have to take our time because we'll be traveling in the dark and won't be able to use the flashlight." He handed her the backpack to use as a pillow again. "And there's always the possibility of a few obstacles along the way like fallen trees or boulders, forcing us to take a detour."

"Remove both of your mittens and take my hand," Sean instructed as he took off his gloves and reached out to Bailey. If she started to fall, he didn't want to risk losing his grip on her if their hands slipped out of a mitten or glove. When she placed her hand in his, he picked up the backpack on the ground beside him and began to inch his way around the fallen boulder that was blocking most of the trail. "Just take your time and you'll be just fine."

It had only been fifteen minutes since they'd left the cave to start down the mountain and they had already encountered a roadblock. They only had a little over twelve inches of path left between the boulder and a drop-off of about twenty feet. If one of them fell here or anywhere else along the trail, they would most likely survive, but not without severe injury and a fair amount of difficulty getting down the mountain to find help without giving themselves away to Crowley. If this was an early indicator of how the trip would go then it didn't bode well.

"This is…a little…harrowing," she said, her breath coming in short puffs. If the death grip she had on his hand was any indication, she wasn't just uneasy about skirting around the boulder, she was downright terrified.

"Breathe slow and steady every time you take a step," he suggested. The last thing he needed was for her to pass out from hyperventilation. When he reached the other side of the boulder, he dropped the backpack, planted his boots firmly on the wider part of the path and prepared to grab her with both hands if she slipped. "You only have a couple of steps and you'll be in the clear, Bailey." He'd no sooner gotten the words out when her foot slid and she fell forward.

"Sean…" His name came out as a cross between a low moan and a loud whisper.

Gripping her hand as tightly as he could,

he felt his shoulder come halfway out of the socket as gravity tried to jerk them both into the dark abyss. He gritted his teeth as he tried to hang on, but she wasn't making it easy, thrashing around for a hand or foothold and pulling him down to his knees. Grabbing her hand with both of his, Sean flattened himself on the ground to try to find the traction he needed to lift her back up to the trail. Every muscle in his upper body strained as he fought to keep from going over the edge with her. In a moment he could tell that he wouldn't be able to do this without her cooperation.

"Bailey, listen to me. I can pull you up, but you're going to have to do something for me."

"W-what?" Her voice was barely audible, but she was still waving her free arm around as she tried to find something to grasp.

"I need you to relax and go perfectly still. Can you do that for me?"

Even in the dark he saw the fear in her eyes as she stared up at him. He was asking her to do something that went completely against human nature. "B-but…"

"I promise I'm not going to let you go." His muscles ached from the prolonged strain and he knew he wouldn't be able to hang on to her for much longer. "But I can't get hold of your other hand like I need to with you moving around like that."

She stared at him for a few seconds longer. "I-I'll…t-try," she said in a broken whisper that just about did him in. In the past couple of days, he'd seen her in tense situations, but this was the first time he'd ever seen her with sheer terror reflected in her expressive green eyes. He hoped with everything in him that it was the last time.

When she stopped moving, he nodded. "Good. Now, don't freak out on me when I turn loose with my left hand and reach for your right arm," he warned. "When I do, I want you to move slow and easy and stretch your arm up toward me as far as you can. I give you my word. I'll take hold of your wrist and you'll be up here on the path beside me in no time."

The tears in her eyes and her trembling lips mouthing an "okay" were like a knife to his gut, but when he reached down, she slowly raised her arm and he grasped her slender right wrist. Slowly crawling back away from the edge, his muscles burned and quivered from the strain and it seemed like it took forever to pull her to safety. But when he finally managed to get Bailey onto solid ground, he released his pent-up breath and pulled her into his arms. Holding her to him, Sean told himself that in comforting her, he was only doing what anyone else would do under the circumstances. But the truth was she'd scared the living daylights out of him and he needed a moment to reassure himself she really was all right.

"It's okay, Bailey," he whispered. "You're safe now. I've got you and you didn't fall. You're all right."

After a few more moments of hugging her and reassuring the both of them that she was safe, he told himself he should release her, stand up and start moving them on down the trail. But she didn't seem to mind him holding on to her a little longer than he should. In fact, she was clinging to him like a baby spider monkey held on to its momma. And he wasn't about to tell her to let go.

You're playing with fire, Hanson. Bailey wasn't looking for anything more from him than keeping her alive. He should be *glad* that was all she was looking for, because even if she wanted more, he wasn't the one she should be setting her sights on. He'd seen too much of the ugly side of life during his years with the Bureau and it had left him feeling a lot older than his thirty-five years. Definitely more jaded than any woman would want to put up with.

"I think we'd better move along," he finally said reluctantly. After releasing her, he stood up then held his hand out to pull her to her feet.

Her tearful gaze met his. "Thank you, Sean. You saved my life. Again." She placed her small, trembling hand in his and even though pain shot through his shoulder as he pulled her to her feet, he refused to let it show. "I don't know how I could possibly repay you for all you've done for me the last couple of days. You're most definitely my hero."

The sincerity in her eyes robbed him of breath. Forcing himself to shake off the sudden need to put his arms around her again, he let go of her soft, delicate hand and cleared the rust from his throat. "No need to thank me."

He wanted to say more, but what? *I like being your hero? I'll be there for you whenever you need me?*

Don't go there, Hanson.

Picking up the backpack, he glanced at her while he shrugged it onto his sore shoulders. He needed to sort out his jumbled feelings and figure out what was wrong with him. In the early days of his career with the FBI, he'd served on security details more times than he could count and he'd never felt toward any of those protectees the way he did with Bailey. He'd never fancied himself a hero to any of them, either. He had taken the responsibility seriously and tried to make them feel that their well-being mattered, that keeping them safe wasn't just something that he had been assigned to do. But wanting to be a hero for any of them had never been an issue.

"I think I owe Blane's foreman's wife a new pair of mittens," Bailey said, looking around. "I can't seem to find them."

"You put them in your coat pocket when you took them off just before we started around the boulder." He couldn't quite look her in the eyes as he picked up his gloves and slipped them on. He needed to understand where his head was at. Once he had his priorities straight, he'd be back on an even keel and better able to keep from making a fool of himself.

"Right. I forgot that after all the…excitement," she murmured.

When she turned to face him, he watched her pull on the mittens, then give him a smile that didn't quite hide the emotions from the ordeal she'd just been through. "I'm ready whenever you are."

Sean nodded. "Hold the cord again like you did when we left the cave and follow me." He waited until she took hold of the short length of paracord he'd attached with a carabiner to the zippered front pocket of the backpack. Once he could feel the light tug of her grip, he slowly started down the dark trail. He'd thought about tying them together but hadn't wanted to drag her off the trail if he was the one who fell.

As they settled into a steady pace, Sean found it almost impossible to relax. It had been a close call—one where he'd almost lost Bailey. A shudder coursed through him at the thought and his gut clenched in a painful knot. No matter what the circumstances, whether it was an obstacle on the trail or the threat of Crowley, he couldn't let that happen again. He tried telling himself that he'd feel that deeply about anyone he was in charge of guarding, but he knew better. Whether he liked it or not, that petite little redhead following him down the mountain was starting to get under his skin in a way he couldn't deny.

He took a deep breath and trudged on down the trail. They had a few miles to go before they found a place to take shelter for the daylight hours. Now, of all times, it was essential that he stay alert.

The distant call of an owl was another reminder that he needed to focus and tune all of his senses into their surroundings. Somewhere on the mountain Crowley was still searching for them, and Sean knew as surely as he knew his own name the bank robber turned killer was going to keep after them until either he was caught or they were killed.

SIX

Bailey followed Sean through the predawn light and wondered what had happened to the man who had saved her life just a few hours ago. He'd become more and more quiet as they made their way down the trail and she wondered if she'd made him uncomfortable when she'd clung to him earlier. Should she apologize for making their situation awkward? She'd thought he'd held on to her just as tightly as she'd hugged him. Or had she mistaken a simple, professional gesture of comfort for something else?

It felt as if he'd erected a wall between them. Was it because she made him feel uneasy or was he simply being cautious and listening for any sound of an ambush or attack?

"We're almost to an overhang where we can hide out until this evening," he said over his shoulder, interrupting her thoughts.

"How are you doing? Still holding up or do we need to stop and rest for a few minutes?"

They'd stopped a couple of times when her leg muscles started cramping from all the unaccustomed exercise. "I'm doing okay," she answered. "I think I can make it until we stop for the day."

"If you're sure…"

"I am." She laughed. "I think I might even be getting accustomed to hiking." The farther they made it down the mountain, the less of an obstacle the snow became. It was amazing what a huge difference it was wading through a foot of snow compared to trudging through *two* feet of the fluffy white stuff.

"You'll be a mountaineer before you know it," he said, sounding amused.

Relieved that it finally felt more like they were on solid ground with each other again, she began to think how different her life had become in the past few days. For as long as she could remember, she'd wished for adventure, to actually live instead of reading about someone else's explorations in a book. But this current escapade wasn't exactly the kind of adventure that she'd had in mind. She'd envisioned long, leisurely walks along the banks of a slow-moving stream or through a forest to see the changing leaves as the trees transformed themselves into vibrant autumn colors. Never in all of her wildest imaginings had she thought she'd be fleeing down a mountain trail throughout the night with a murderous bank robber in hot pursuit.

Suddenly, there was an odd-sounding crack and one of the boughs on the tree beside her exploded into a shower of pine needles and bark. "What in the world…?"

"We're under fire!" Scan whirled around, grabbed her at the waist and dragged her into the dense stand of trees along the trail. Once he had them crouched behind a huge Douglas fir tree, he held her to his side and whispered close to her ear. "The shot came from the cliff just above us and to the right."

"How did he find us?" As the reality of the situation started to sink in, her hands began to tremble and she felt like someone had punched her in the stomach. If the shot had been a fraction of an inch to the right, she would have been killed.

"My guess is they split up. One of them is on the west side of the mountain and the other is on this side."

"It was so close," she murmured. "Just a little farther over, and I…" She shuddered with fear in spite of herself.

Tightening his arm around her, he kissed the top of her head, then tucked her head beneath his chin. "Don't think about it, Bailey. Whether it was by an inch or a mile, he missed. That's all that matters."

She nodded. But for the life of her, she couldn't force words past her cold, paralyzed lips. Another bullet whizzed past them and landed with a dull *thunk* in the trunk of a tree behind them. She swallowed her panicked squeak and burrowed deeper into Sean's embrace.

Pulling her upright, Sean moved them quickly between several trees before he stopped to crouch behind another large trunk. "We're going to plan B. We'll have to take another route through the forest to get down to the valley." He paused for a moment. "I'm sorry, but we won't be stopping to rest until we reach the valley this evening. We'll just have to keep going."

When he stood, he brought her up with him. "Since it's light enough for you to see, you don't need to hold on to the backpack. I do, however, need you to stay close and in front of me."

"O-kay."

He reached out as if he intended to touch her face when there was another crack, another shower of pine needles from a bough close by. Quickly reaching for her hand, he urged her along. "We're going to make it out of this," he said as they jogged as fast as the snow allowed through the dense trees for several minutes. When he stopped for her to catch her breath, he caught her gaze with his. "I want you to promise me something, Bailey."

"What?" she asked, looking up at his handsome face.

"If something does happen to me or if we get separated, I want you to keep running and don't look back." When she started to protest, he shook his head. "Stick to the trees and move in a zigzag fashion. It'll make you harder to hit. You'll eventually come to a road about two miles down the mountain. Stay within the tree line and follow it to the east. It will take you a couple of hours walking, but it leads into the valley. Keep going until you see a little building at the end of the valley, sitting at the bottom of a cliff. Hide there and wait for Blane and Levi to arrive. I'll try to get hold of them to let them know you'll be there by early evening instead of tomorrow morning."

As she thought about doing what he asked,

something inside her snapped. "Absolutely not!"

He blinked. "Say what?"

Her vehemence even took *her* by surprise, but she wasn't going to consider any scenario where she ran off and left him behind if he was shot or injured in some way. "Let me tell you something right here and now, Sean Hanson. I am not about to leave you bleeding in the snow while I run off like a scared rabbit trying to find a hole to hide in. You're just not going to get shot. Or hurt. Period. You're going to stay upright, mobile and as healthy as the proverbial horse and we're both going to make it off this mountain alive. Together. You got that straight, cowboy?"

He stared at her for a few seconds and just when she thought he was going to tell her she'd crossed a line, a slow grin spread across his face. "Yes, ma'am."

"Good. Now let's get going before that horrible man catches up to us." She had no idea what had gotten into her or where all of her determination came from. She'd never talked to anyone like that in her life and she was a little embarrassed by her outburst. But she couldn't stand the thought of something happening to him and it had felt good to speak her mind for a change instead of clamming up and accepting the status quo.

She wasn't going to fool herself into thinking that it was just because she needed him to guide her to safety. No, it went deeper than that. For the first time in her life, she was on her own and completely independent. She was still in the discovery stage, trying to find out who she was and what direction she wanted her life to take and she just wasn't sure she'd be ready now or in the near future to accept the real reason she was so intent on keeping Sean safe.

Sean set a brisk pace as they followed a deer trail through the trees on their way down the mountain. If he was correct and the shot had come from the cliff above them, it would take a while for the shooter to make his way down to the trail. He wanted to take advantage of the time that would give them and cover as much distance as they could. If they were fast enough, maybe the timing would work out to keep the shooter from being able to figure out what trail they'd taken altogether. The last thing he wanted was to lead the shooter to the valley where his brothers would be meeting them. He was going to have to call Blane and let him and

Levi know about the revised ETA, but he wanted to wait to make the call until after they'd started down the road into the valley. There were a couple of very good reasons for that. For one, finding a strong radio wave from a passing communications satellite while on the mountain wasn't always guaranteed, thanks to interference from the topography and the thick tree canopy. The closer they got to the valley, the better chance he had of locking on to a clear, unobstructed signal. And the second reason was he wanted to use this time to get as far away from Crowley as they could possibly get.

As he followed Bailey, Sean couldn't keep from smiling as he replayed her outburst over and over in his mind. She'd startled him with her off-the-cuff speech and he was pretty sure she'd surprised herself, as well. She was without a doubt one of the most fascinating women he'd ever had the pleasure of meeting. And after her fiery objections to the mere idea of his getting hurt, it was harder than ever to push away the thoughts of caring for her, having her care for him.

He frowned. What was he thinking, anyway? Why on earth would a woman as young and vivacious as Bailey be interested in a used-up old Fed like himself? He might only be thirty-five, but there were times, when he was reminded of some of the cases he'd worked, that left him feeling like he was at least a hundred and thirty-five. The things people did in fits of rage or came up with in order to cause harm to others, were impossible to forget, no matter how hard he tried. They'd left their stains on his mind and his heart—maybe even on his soul. He had no right to subject anyone else to the darkness he now carried inside him.

"Sean, could we stop…for a couple of minutes?" Bailey asked, sounding a little winded.

"Of course." More than ready to get his mind off his former career and the way it had damaged him, he quickly spotted a fallen log in a thick stand of spruce trees and, placing his hand to her back, steered her toward it. "Let's rest over here."

When he was satisfied they were hidden from view on all sides, he offered her a drink of water as they sat down. "How much farther do we have to go before we get to the road?" she asked, taking a sip from the bottle.

"We're within an hour of it." He checked his watch. "We should get there in time to have a late lunch before we start down into the valley."

She gave him a teasing grin. "What's on the menu for today? Dare I hope it's granola bars and water?"

"Oh you're in for a treat. We have gourmet fare today," he said, liking their easy banter. "I happen to have teriyaki-flavored beef jerky and a fine *botella de agua* in my backpack for your dining pleasure."

His comment drew out the soft sound of her laughter as he hoped it would. "If my high school Spanish is correct that's a bottle of water, sir."

"Yeah, and that's about the extent of my Spanish," Sean admitted, smiling. He stood up to stretch his sore back and shoulder muscles. A quiet yet ominous sound like a purring cat caught his attention and, looking up, he spotted just about the last thing he wanted to see up in the trees. "Bailey, do me a favor," he said, careful to keep his voice even and calm.

"Sure. What do you need?"

"Get up and slowly move over here with me," he said, never taking his eyes off the big, tawny-colored cat lying on a limb about twenty-five feet above Bailey's head. The way the cougar eyed her, Sean was pretty sure it wanted to make her its next meal.

"What are you looking at?" she asked as she walked over to stand beside him. He knew the moment she looked up and saw the mountain lion. "Oh no! Sean, that's a—" Her words came to an abrupt halt when the animal opened its mouth and let loose with a typical cougar scream that could raise the hair on the head of a bald man.

When Bailey let loose with a startled cry and whirled around to run, he caught her by the arm. "Stay right beside me," he said in a low voice. "Running will make him want to chase after you. Just stay beside me and do what I tell you."

"O-okay."

"Unsnap the holster on the left side of my belt, take out the spray can and hand it to me," he instructed, never dropping eye contact with the big cat. When she handed him the canister of bear spray, he quickly used his thumb to remove the safety tab and held the trigger grip at the ready. "Now unbutton your coat, raise your arms above your head to make yourself appear as big and tall as you can and start yelling as loud as possible."

"But I thought we were trying to stay

quiet to keep our location concealed," she said, even as she opened her coat, then stretched her arms high.

"Yeah, forget that. Crowley isn't our biggest threat right now." He made himself as big as he could, as well, then nodded toward the limb as the lion raised itself to a crouch. "He is."

"Right."

"On three. One, two, three," he counted.

Together they both started shouting and moving their arms in menacing gestures. He was hoping the animal would decide that they were more trouble than what they were worth.

After a solid minute of making enough noise to wake the dead, it became clear the cat wasn't intimidated in the least by their efforts. "Okay, he's not buying what we're selling." Sean held the bear spray at the ready. "Time for us to start backing away. Move slowly—take it one step at a time without lowering your arms or breaking eye contact."

By the time the cougar jumped they had managed to move a good fifteen feet from where he landed. As the cat started toward them, Sean shoved Bailey behind him, took aim and pulled the trigger on the bear repel-

lent. The animal stopped, let loose a stran-
gled cry that sounded otherworldly, then
turned and ran away like its tail was on fire.

Without delay, Sean took her hand and
urged her to start down the slope at a brisk
pace in the opposite direction just in case
the cougar changed its mind.

"Is he...following...us?" she asked, sounding like she was running a marathon.

Realizing they had been jogging for some
distance, he slowed them to a walk. "I'd say
he's too busy scrubbing at his eyes and nose
with his paws to worry about us."

"Will he be...all right?" She looked worried. "I don't want him to have any lasting
problems or anything."

"You don't have to worry about that big
boy. He just has a temporary burning problem with his eyes and nasal passages, but
otherwise he'll be fine."

They were silent for a time while they
continued down the slope.

"We're about a hundred yards or so from
the road." He checked his watch. They were
a bit earlier than he had estimated, which
wasn't surprising given how they'd hustled
to escape the mountain lion. "I should be
able to get hold of at least one of my brothers now."

"What happens if you can't reach them?"

He couldn't blame her for asking. Every time they'd thought they had things worked out something came along to derail their plans.

"If I can't get hold of them, we'll stay at the line shack until morning. That's where we were supposed to meet them, anyway. We'll just have to spend a little more time waiting." He pointed to a grouping of boulders a few yards ahead of them on the edge of the lane. "Let's stop there. You can rest while I try to get hold of Blane or Levi."

Bailey listened as Sean talked to his brother, Levi. It wasn't that she was trying to eavesdrop, but when he was standing barely ten feet away, it was hard not to overhear at least one side of the conversation.

Sean must have realized that, given what he said when he rejoined her. "I guess you heard that it will be close to midnight before they can get up here to pick us up?" he asked, rubbing the back of his neck with his gloved hand.

She nodded. "What happened?"

"Apparently, Crowley has more than one person working with him. While he was up here on the mountain, chasing after us, one of his cohorts decided to make sure my brothers were so busy dealing with catastrophes of their own, they wouldn't be available to help us." His dark scowl turned thunderous as he removed his backpack and handed her a bottle of water and a package of beef jerky. After they held hands for a quick prayer, he explained. "Levi spent half of the day trying to round up two hundred head of cattle that mysteriously got out of the pasture behind his house and ended up wandering all the way over to Thad's place. Thad was helping Levi round up the herd when he discovered one of the stables was on fire."

She sucked in a sharp breath. "Oh no! Please tell me no one was hurt—not your brothers or the animals."

"No, but he lost a lot of feed and tack, not to mention the expense he'll now face of replacing the new stable and indoor arena we all worked on a year ago this past summer."

"What about Blane? Was his section of the ranch damaged in any way?" She couldn't help but think that the Hanson brothers had suffered so much—personally and financially—because of Sean helping her.

"Every tire on every one of the ranch trucks, tractors, hay balers and wagons was slashed. And the hose was cut on the fuel tank he uses to refuel the equipment."

"I feel so guilty," she said, catching her lower lip between her teeth. She set down the package of jerky he'd given her and the bottle of water and twisted her hands into a tight knot. "If it wasn't for you and your family helping me, none of you would have had to deal with any of this."

Sean squatted down in front of her and took her mittened hands in his. "None of this is your fault, Bailey. This is Crowley's desperate attempt to delay the inevitable. The Bureau will catch him, the courts will convict him and the prison system will incarcerate him for the rest of his sorry life and there's nothing he can do to stop that." He squeezed her hands encouragingly. "And if the truth is known, he's after me more than he is you."

"Why on earth would you think that?" she asked. "I'm the one who can identify him as the bank robber."

Sean took a deep breath. "Day before yesterday's heist was far from his first bank robbery. Crowley and I have history. I negotiated a hostage situation he was involved in a few years back."

When he paused, she could tell there was

more to the story, but she could also see that he was reluctant to share it. And from the look on his face, she wasn't sure she wanted to know what he was leaving out. Her nightmares were already bad enough. Learning more about the terrible things Crowley had done was hardly going to make her feel better.

"So what happens now?" she asked, feeling a cold chill slither up her spine that had nothing to do with the temperature.

He stared at her for several long moments and just when she thought he was going to reach to take her into his arms, he stood up and looked away. "We're going to proceed as planned and head to the line shack. We can't build a fire in the stove or light one of the kerosene lanterns, but at least we can hole up in there and get out of the wind until Blane and Levi can get there."

"Do you think Harold Crowley and whoever is with him heard us earlier?" she asked, looking around. "Could they know where we are or where this shack is?"

"It's possible, but I doubt it. They couldn't know everything about this mountain because it's privately owned."

"But they knew just where to go for your

cabin and found which trail we took to come down the mountain."

"I've been thinking about that, too," he admitted. "You'd almost think they had our GPS coordinates."

"Could they be tracking your phone?" If the crime shows she'd watched were accurate, his cell phone might have been the culprit.

"I don't think so." He pulled it from his coat pocket. "I don't have a phone with one of the national carriers. I always use a prepaid phone and replace it after the minutes have been used up."

"Why?" she asked, genuinely confused by what seemed to her an overabundance of caution.

He shrugged. "I got into the habit of using burner phones when I worked undercover or on high-profile cases. It seemed like a better option than destroying an expensive phone if for some reason my identity was compromised or I needed to drop off the grid. Plus, it keeps me in the habit of not storing a lot of personal data on my phone. If someone manages to swipe it, they won't be able to get much of my info from it."

She'd never thought of that, but in his line of work, it made perfect sense. "Well, they can't track me through the GPS on my phone because I was told by the Men in Black of the Wyoming Highway Patrol to leave my phone at home."

The sound of his deep laughter set the butterflies in her stomach to fluttering wildly. "They *did* look like they could be in search of UFOs and little green men, didn't they?"

She smiled. "They really did."

"But that leaves us with the problem of how Crowley has been right behind us every step of the way," he said, his smile fading. He stared at her for a moment before he asked, "Are you wearing the coat you wore to the bank before it was robbed—the one you had to pick up at the sheriff's office?"

"It's the only heavy coat I have," she admitted. "After living here for a couple of months, I'm beginning to think I might need to have one a little more on the practical side instead of going for something stylish. This isn't nearly as warm as I wish it was."

He took off his coat and held it out to her. "Could you do me a favor and wear my coat for a minute or two while I check out yours?"

She couldn't imagine what he thought he'd find, but slipping out of her classic black, wool peacoat, she put on his. Just like the first time he'd wrapped her up in the suede-and-sherpa jacket, she felt surrounded by him, his scent and his strength. Her heart skipped a beat and she had to remind herself that Sean was only with her in order to see that a dangerous man paid his debt to society. He was just doing his job and when that was done and Harold Crowley was locked away for the rest of his miserable life, she'd most likely never see Sean again. But it was probably for the best. She was still trying to find who she was and what she wanted from life.

"Just as I suspected," he said, bringing her back to the present. He pulled a tiny buttonlike pin from under the back collar of her coat and showed it to her. "A standard government-issue personal GPS tracking device."

"That was on my coat all this time?" It gave her a creepy feeling that someone had invaded her privacy in that way, especially when that person was almost certainly a corrupt federal agent tracking her location so that a killer could find her.

"Yes, and I'd say whoever is working with Crowley planted that on your coat the night they returned it to the sheriff's office." His frown turned into a fierce scowl. "It has to be someone who knows me well enough to know how close I am to my brothers. The other day in the truck, Blane wasn't joking when he said that messing with one Hanson meant you had to deal with all of us. That's how they knew to vandalize the ranch to try and stop my brothers from helping us."

Bailey couldn't help but be in awe of the Hanson family. They were everything she would want her own family to be, if she'd had one. "But it's not going to work, is it? All Crowley and his cohort succeeded in doing was to make your brothers all the more determined to help you put them in jail."

"Yup. They thought if my brothers were busy dealing with their own problems they wouldn't have the time to help us with ours. But that's not the way we roll. The repairs around the ranch can wait. A family member in need of help is top priority."

She removed his jacket to hand it back to him. "How long will it take to get to the shack?"

"We're making better time than I expected so we should arrive on the other end of the valley by late afternoon." He held her coat for her while she slipped her arms into the sleeves, then shrugging into his jacket, he took the GPS device he'd removed from under her coat collar and, stepping to the other side of the trail, threw it into a deep ravine. "By the time they climb down to the bottom of that gorge looking for us and then back up to try and figure out where we went, we'll be well on the way to the line shack and the snowstorm that's moving in should have covered up our tracks."

As she followed him through the trees along the side of the dirt road, she hoped getting rid of the tracker stopped the criminals from following them. But deep down she couldn't help but feel like that was wishful thinking. Crowley was a desperate and very determined man. She just hoped that Sean's brothers arrived to evacuate them before the bank robber found them and carried out his plans to eliminate her once and for all.

SEVEN

When Sean opened the door to the one-room shack and ushered Bailey inside, he was relieved to see it was still in fairly good shape and surprisingly varmint-free. Racoons were cute from a distance, but they could be real mean little critters when they felt cornered and a mother with kits was every bit as ferocious as a momma bear with a couple of cubs.

"It's not a mansion by any stretch of the imagination, but it's dry and will keep us out of the wind and snow until the cavalry arrives."

He watched her look around at the meager furnishings in the small room. "I have one question. What is a line shack used for?"

"In the mid-to-late 1800s and early 1900s, they were used as a temporary shelter for cowboys who had to ride a good distance away from the ranch headquarters to check on herds of cattle and to ride along the property line fences to make repairs," he explained, dusting off the chair at the small table for her to sit down. He'd noticed the last hour of their trek across the valley that she'd started to slow down and looked thoroughly exhausted.

She smiled as she sat on the chair. "In other words, a cowboy on some ranch way back in the 'good old days' was the first occupant of a 'tiny house.'"

"I hadn't thought of it that way, but I guess you're right," he said, grinning as he looked around at the interior of the little building. He was pretty sure the walk-in closet in his bedroom was bigger.

"I do have a suggestion for the decor," she said, her smile mischievous. "If you want to take the charm factor up a notch from shabby to rustic chic, you could always add some ruffled calico curtains to the windows and a braided rug in front of that little-bitty stove."

He laughed. "It sounds like we might need to hire you to decorate the place."

He found that he really liked listening to her observations. They were clever and amusing and he was charmed by the way she found lightness and humor in every situation. It was just one more thing he liked about her. But it wasn't in his best interest to dwell on her quick wit and charming personality. She was full of life and wonder and wouldn't have any place in her life for a man who was content to spend his time hidden out on a mountain quietly taking pictures of wildlife and mountain scenery.

Still smiling, she tilted her head. "You have a nice laugh, Sean. You should do it more often."

Her compliment caught him off guard and caused his heart to pound against his ribs. How long had it been since a woman had caused him to feel like a teenage boy with his first crush? But even though he couldn't stop himself from responding to her, it didn't change anything. Nothing could ever come of the longing to have someone special in his life and he might as well accept it and move on.

Unable to find anything to say that wouldn't betray his inner struggle, he shrugged off the backpack, set it on the table and opening it, took out the flannel blanket they had used to sit on inside the cave. Spreading it over the mattress on the narrow cot against the wall, he figured it would protect her from the dust if she wanted to stretch out for a while.

"Feel free to take a nap," he offered, also removing the space blanket from the pack. It was still extremely frigid, even though they were inside the shack. But they didn't dare start a fire in the small stove in the corner for fear of giving away their location, and she would need something over her to keep her body temperature up. "I know you're cold and tired and it's been almost twenty-four hours since you slept last."

She stood up to stretch but ended up shivering, just as he'd expected. Still, she tried to argue as she stepped close to him, poking a finger against his chest for emphasis. "You have to be just as beat as I am, if not more so. You've been awake longer and pulling me to safety after I slipped and fell off the trail must have been exhausting. Go ahead and get some sleep. I'll take my turn in a couple of hours."

"Bailey, I appreciate your thoughtfulness." He decided he couldn't stand to see her shivering, right in front of him, without doing something about it. Opening the lapels of his coat, he put his arms around her and pulled her close to share his body heat. "But I need to stay awake to watch for anyone approaching the shack."

"I could watch and if I see something,

wake you up." She covered a yawn with her delicate hand as she rested her forehead on his chest. "Just tell me what to look for."

Tucking her head beneath his chin, he smiled. "I appreciate your offer, as well as your concern for me, but I'll sleep after Blane and Levi pick us up and get us to someplace safe."

When she remained silent and began to sag against him, he laughed quietly as he scooped her up and carried her the few feet to the cot. He'd been right about her being tired. She'd fallen asleep standing up. After he gently laid her on the flannel, he covered her with the space blanket, then looked out the grimy windows to make sure no one was prowling around outside the little shanty.

Everything looked all right, but Crowley was still out there, working with an unknown number of accomplices.

Glancing over at her sleeping form on the narrow cot, he couldn't help but think about how pretty she was and how much he loathed Crowley for terrorizing her. He was determined to see to it that the criminal was never again in the position to menace Bailey or any other woman. He was more than ready to be done with Crowley. But the end of the danger would also bring an end to his time with the most captivating woman he'd ever met.

Get over it, Hanson. You'd do well to spend more time focusing on how to keep her safe and less on how much you'd like to just plain keep her.

Bailey slowly became aware of the muffled sound of men talking and realized they were just outside the door. Cautiously sitting up, she immediately realized that Sean wasn't there, even though it was so dark she could barely see the interior of the line shack. His brothers had probably arrived and he had stepped out to talk to them. When her eyes adjusted to the darkened room, she could see through the dirty windows that it was nighttime and that the moon and stars had come out after it stopped snowing.

She felt guilty for sleeping so long and failing to give Sean a chance to rest. But he hadn't awakened her and she really wasn't surprised that he hadn't. He seemed to think she was some kind of delicate creature that needed to be taken care of, while he was completely invincible. That was something that would have to be addressed. While she was flattered and grateful that he was protective of her, she couldn't allow him to look after her to the detriment of his own needs. He had missed more sleep than she had and had to be physically exhausted from everything he'd brought her through. Not to mention, he'd been splitting the food and water with her right down the middle even though with his height and muscle mass, he was certain to need more calories than she did.

As she sat there on the side of the cot, wondering why he thought her safety and comfort were more important than his own, the door opened and the object of her speculation walked inside. "Are your brothers here?"

"They arrived about ten minutes ago," he said, nodding.

She stood up and started folding the space blanket. "Why didn't you wake me earlier so you could get some sleep, as well?"

"I'm used to operating on very little sleep when I'm on an assignment," he said, taking the folded silver material from her to store in the backpack. "I can't do it forever, of course, but I can get by for a couple of days."

"That may be so, but…"

He stepped in front of her and tipped her chin up until their gazes met. "I'll be fine as long as you're safe and out of harm's way."

The tender expression on his handsome

face and the sincerity in his dark brown eyes caused her to feel warm all over. Sean was one of the kindest, most decent men she'd ever had the privilege to meet. Before she could respond, Blane and another man she assumed to be their brother Levi, entered the shack and closed the door quietly behind them.

"We've got company," Blane said in a low voice.

Sean pulled his Kevlar vest from the backpack to drape it over her shoulders. "It's not the right size, but since we're putting it on top of your coat, this might not be too big on you." He adjusted the Velcro fasteners on the shoulders and sides of the heavy vest, then turned to his brothers. "Where are they?"

The man she assumed to be Levi spoke up. "On the west side of the valley a little over three hundred yards out."

"We need to get out of here and down to the truck," Sean said, grabbing the flannel blanket from the bed and stuffing it into his backpack. "Blane, you take the lead. Levi, you bring up the rear and be sure to watch your six."

Levi grinned. "Always do, big brother."

Blane opened the door. "Ready or not, let's do this."

"Bailey, I want you between me and Blane," Sean said as they stepped out into the night.

She nodded and followed Blane as they crept away from the shack toward the tree line fifty yards away. When they reached it, she saw a path that led down through the birch trees away from the upland valley. Thankful they'd made it to the safety of the woods, she had just breathed a sigh of relief when a crack suddenly split the air. She heard Sean grunt in pain and fall to the ground behind her.

"Sean!" Bailey spun around and started to kneel beside him but Blane caught her by the waist and, whirling her around, scooped her up into his arms bridal style and carried her down the path into the trees at a quick pace. She struggled to free herself from his iron grip. "No, Blane! We have to help Sean! He's been shot. We have to go back!"

"Levi is with him," Blane said as he ran with her down the trail. When she continued to try to break free, he set her down and urged her along ahead of him. "Sean will kill me if I do anything *other* than get you away from here. I promise you, Levi will take care of whatever happened to Sean."

Not at all satisfied with his answer, she

planted her feet and caused Blane to stumble to a stop to keep from running over her. "I refuse to take another step until we go back to see about Sean."

"Bailey, I understand you're concerned about him. Believe me, I am, too. But he made me promise that if something happened to him, I would get you to safety no matter what." When she started to run past him, he scooped her up once more and started down the winding path through the trees. "Forgive me, but Sean gave me a specific order and I'm going to follow it to the letter."

Tears blurred her vision as Blane whisked her farther away from Sean, not stopping until he reached a parked truck. When he set her on her feet again, she caught sight of Sean and Levi jogging down the path toward them.

Thank You, dear God, for keeping him alive.

She took a step toward him. "I thought you were shot."

"I'm fine," he said, wrapping his right arm around her. He held her close for a moment, then led her over to the truck. "Let's get out of here before Crowley catches up with us."

As she scrambled up into the truck she noticed that Sean stepped back and had Blane help her before he hurriedly got into the backseat beside her. His brothers climbed into the front and just as Levi started the truck and put it into gear the back window shattered and pieces of glass rained down on her and Sean. His arm shot out to pull her head down toward her lap while he covered her with his body, asking, "Are you all right? Are you hurt anywhere? Do you have any cuts?"

"Not that I'm aware of," she said as Levi stomped on the gas, spraying gravel and snow as he fishtailed the truck onto the road to speed away. "What about you?"

"Nothing but the flesh wound where I was shot," he said so casually that she thought for a second that she might have misunderstood him. How could he be so unconcerned about something as serious as a gunshot wound?

"You were shot," she accused, struggling against him to sit up. "Where?" Just the thought of him being injured because of her, made her feel sick inside.

"It's nothing major, honestly. Just a flesh wound. No big deal."

"Don't tell me it's nothing. Any gunshot wound should be taken seriously. Where did the bullet hit you?" She looked at the front of his coat then turned her attention to the sleeves. His right arm looked all right, but his left arm had a tear on the upper part of the suede sleeve and a moist, dark red stain that had seeped through the material. Tears filled her eyes. "Oh, Sean… I'm so…sorry."

"Honest, Bailey, I'm fine." He pulled her to him and held her with his right arm. "As soon as we get to Levi's place, I'll have him tend to it, stitch it up if it needs it, put some antibiotic salve on it and I'll be good as new."

She leaned back to look at him. "Is he qualified to do that?"

Laughing, Sean nodded. "I know he doesn't look smart enough for it, but he was a corpsman for his entire eight-year stint in the navy. And now he's the head of the Search and Rescue Team in Eagle Fork. He's certified and licensed as a paramedic nationally and in the state of Wyoming."

"Don't worry, Bailey," Levi said from the driver's seat as he slowed the truck down for a hairpin turn. "He'll be fine. I've patched up him and my other two boneheaded brothers more times than I care to count and they're all still alive and kickin'."

"Hey, who are you calling boneheaded?" Blane asked, good-naturedly.

Feeling guilty for the way she'd physically lashed out at Blane in her effort to get back to Sean, she cleared her throat. "Uh, Blane? I'm really sorry I gave you so much trouble earlier," she apologized.

He smiled at her over his shoulder. "Don't worry about it, Bailey. I know you were concerned about Sean and I don't blame you one bit."

"Thank you, Blane." She took a deep breath and rested her head against Sean's shoulder. "How long before we get to Levi's place?"

"We're about twenty minutes away," Sean answered, pulling her a little closer.

"Where are we going to hide out after your brother takes care of your arm?" she asked, wondering if they were going to have to be on the run forever, never able to get more than a few steps ahead of Crowley.

"I'm not sure." He leaned his cheek against her head. "But I promise, I'll make sure it's somewhere safe."

"It looks like you're going to need some staples to close the trench that bullet plowed through the outside of your upper arm," Levi said, flushing the wound with saline.

Sitting at his brother's kitchen table, Sean watched Levi reach for the surgical stapler. "Why aren't you using stitches?"

"Staples aren't as easy to tear loose as stitches, so they are the best choice for your arm, especially since I know you're going to ignore medical advice about taking it easy while you heal." Levi pinched the two sides of the torn skin together, then lining up the medical stapler, gently squeezed the device to eject the first staple into Sean's skin. "Just moving your arm at the elbow or shoulder will put stress on the wound, and I wouldn't advise picking up anything heavier than five pounds with this arm until it's healed and the staples are removed."

"You tell him, Doc," Blane said, grinning as he entered the kitchen. "If he doesn't behave we can always get Dr. Dolittle to patch him up." Since Thad had received his doctorate in veterinary medicine, they'd all started referring to their youngest brother by the legendary veterinarian's name.

"Where's Bailey?" Sean didn't like having her out of his sight for long, considering how fast things had gone sideways at other times when they should have been safe.

"She said she wanted to take a shower, so I showed her where the guest bedroom is and told her she could use the adjoining bathroom," Blane answered as he walked over to the coffeepot to get a cup of freshly brewed coffee. "When I left her, she was digging through your backpack and muttering something about a toothbrush and a pair of socks."

Remembering Bailey's conversation with his brother on the way to Levi's, he asked, "What happened while you were getting her to the truck that she felt the need to apologize?"

Blane's wide grin suddenly made Sean wish he hadn't asked. "That little lady came real close to going all momma bear on me when I was trying to get her to leave you behind after you were shot. I ended up having to pick her up and carry her to the truck because she was determined to go back to see if you were all right."

Sean laughed. "She certainly doesn't suffer from a lack of determination. She chewed me out when I tried to tell her that if something happened to me, I wanted her to run and not look back."

"Sounds to me like she's as sweet on you

as you are on her," Levi said, shooting another staple into Sean's arm.

Sean whipped his head around to glare at his brother. "Nobody's sweet on anybody," he stated firmly. "I'm in charge of keeping her safe and she's too young for me, anyway."

Levi stopped shooting staples into his arm to stare at him like he'd sprouted another head. "How old is she? She looked to me to be somewhere in her midtwenties. That's not too young."

"She's twenty-five," Sean answered, wishing that he'd kept his mouth shut in the first place.

"Mom is ten years younger than Dad," Blane pointed out. "And I don't think there has ever been two people more perfect for each other. They're still like a couple of love-struck teenagers. You'd think that now they're retired and spending all their time together, they'd welcome a break from each other every now and then, but that just isn't the case."

"That's different."

"How?" Blane and Levi asked at the same time.

"Mom was twenty and Dad was almost thirty-one when they got together," Levi said, shooting the last staple into Sean's skin. "And the last time I was down in Arizona for a visit, they didn't want to be out of the other's sight."

"Kind of like he and Bailey are now," Blane added, grinning like a deranged hyena.

Sean clenched his teeth until his jaw throbbed. "If you two don't lay off..."

"What's going on?" Bailey asked, entering the kitchen from the hall. When he and his brothers remained silent, she walked directly over to Sean to inspect the wound on his left arm. The tears that filled her eyes when she looked at him just about did him in. "I hate that you were hurt because of me."

Levi coughed and Blane choked on his coffee as they tried to cover their laughter. Sean knew beyond a shadow of a doubt that they were dying to say something and that they probably wouldn't be able to hold themselves back for long.

"Blane, don't you think we need to go check in with the guys patrolling the perimeter?" Levi asked as he finished wrapping gauze around Sean's arm. Blane had brought some of his cowboys over to help at Levi's and they'd set up makeshift guard stations in strategic locations all around the house and barns as the first line of defense in case Crowley wanted to come calling.

"Yeah, checking in to see how things are going would probably be a good idea," Blane agreed, his cheesy grin grating on Sean's already irritated nerves. "Besides, it is pretty late and you know how these old guys are. Methuselah here probably needs a nap or something."

Levi threw back his head and laughed so hard, Sean thought his brother might pass out. It would serve him right if he did, he thought sourly.

"Am I missing something?" Bailey asked, looking confused as she placed her hand on his shoulder.

"We were just giving the old man here a hard time," Levi said, wiping his eyes.

"Old man?" She shook her head. "I've never considered thirty-five to be old."

Blane and Levi both wore irritating smirks when they said almost in unison, "Told you so, Methuselah."

"Will you two get out of here and check to make sure Crowley hasn't shown up?" Sean muttered. He was extremely conscious of his brothers' attention on the way Bailey's hand rested on his shoulder. For that matter, it had his attention, as well. The warmth from her palm through the cotton T-shirt he'd borrowed from Levi spread throughout his chest and he wasn't sure he ever wanted her to move it.

"I didn't cause a problem between you and your brothers, did I?" she asked as Levi and Blane reached for their coats and headed out the back door.

She looked so concerned, he rose to his feet and wrapped his arms around her. "Don't worry about me and my brothers. We pick at each other and bicker back and forth just to have something to do. Believe me, I turn it around and needle them about stuff every chance I get."

"I don't know much about that type of family dynamic." She put her arms around his waist and rested her cheek on his chest.

He stood there holding her for several long moments, wondering what he could do to bring back her smile. "Would you like to call your parents to let them know what's going on? Crowley is already aware of our location and they are far enough away that it won't jeopardize their safety. I'm sure they'd be glad to hear from you, to get an update on what's going on."

"I really wish… I could."

Her words were barely audible and leaning back, he placed his index finger under her chin and tipped her head back until their eyes met. The sadness in her emerald gaze caused his stomach to twist into a tight knot.

He tucked a strand of her long copper hair behind her ear. "Did something happen that caused a rift in your relationship with them?"

A pair of tears spilled from her eyes and slowly made their way down her cheeks before she shook her head and looked away. "My dad died from an undiagnosed congenital heart defect when I was twelve, and my mother passed away back in January from complications of a stroke she suffered two years ago."

Sean winced, sorry that he'd brought up what was clearly a painful subject. "Is there someone else you want to contact? An aunt or uncle? Maybe a cousin?" he asked, hoping there was someone.

She shook her head. "There's…no one."

He'd never in a million years expected to learn that she was completely alone in the world. Tightening his arms around her, he felt her tremble as she sobbed against his shirt. She was bone tired, scared by the threats of a ruthless criminal and missing the people who had loved her the most. "I'm so sorry, Bailey."

He'd comforted emotional women before when he had to inform them that someone they cared about had lost their life, either by accident or at the hands of someone else. But that was different. Those women weren't Bailey. Her tears caused his chest to tighten and his stomach to twist as if someone had punched him in the gut.

"It's going to be all right," he whispered against her hair. "You're safe with me and I swear I won't let anyone hurt you."

"I know you won't, but please don't put yourself in danger because of me," she said, looking up at him. "I couldn't live with that if something happened to you or your brothers while you were trying to protect me."

"And I couldn't live with myself if I let something happen to you. I guess the only thing we can do is both stay out of the line of fire and not get hurt."

"That sounds like a good plan to me," she said, staring up at him.

Her tears had made her lashes spiky and her eyes darken from Kelly green to forest green. She was absolutely stunning and he couldn't have stopped himself from lowering his head to press his mouth to hers if his life depended on it.

Her lips were soft and perfect and his heart hammered hard against his rib cage when she kissed him back. The caress didn't last long, but that didn't make it any less sweet.

Or any less of a mistake. Knowing how little he had to offer her, Sean knew he had no right to kiss her. And yet, he couldn't bring himself to apologize or say it was a mistake. He wasn't sorry—and nothing in his life had ever felt so right.

Raising his head, Sean stepped back and cleared his suddenly dry throat. "I, uh, should probably get hold of Sam Fowler and update him on the situation. He needs to know that our location was compromised and that we're on the other side of the mountain at Levi's."

She nodded. "Do you have any idea where we're going to go once we leave here? We obviously can't stay for long. We'd be putting your brothers in danger."

"As soon as they come back inside, I'm going to talk with them and get their take on the situation." He couldn't resist touching her again and reaching out, traced his finger down the satin-smooth skin of her cheek.

"There's still a few hours left before dawn. Why don't you try to get some more sleep?"

"Why don't you?" she challenged, tilting her head and looking at him the way women did when they want to make a point—and he had to admit that she had a good one here.

He needed to put some distance between them and regain his perspective. He couldn't help but feel that he was teetering on the edge of something and he wasn't overly confident about which way he would fall. Part of the problem might be that he was running on adrenaline, which was definitely not a good way to keep a clear head. He needed some time to rest, to process, to sort himself out. But before that could happen, he needed to talk to his brothers and put together a plan. He couldn't rest easy until he knew their next steps were in place.

"I promise I'll get some rest as soon as I talk to my brothers and get ahold of Sam." He walked her down the hall to the guest bedroom and stopped at the door.

To his surprise, she wrapped her arms around his waist and gave him a quick hug. Then, without a word, she went into the bedroom and closed the door.

When he walked back into the kitchen, he grabbed a mug from the cabinet above the coffee maker and poured himself a cup of coffee. What in the world had he done?

He rubbed the tension building at the base of his neck. She hadn't objected to his kiss. In fact, she'd kissed him back and that opened up a whole new can of worms. All of this time, he'd been telling himself that she deserved someone a whole lot better than the likes of him. What could he offer a woman like her, anyway? She certainly wouldn't want a man who occasionally suffered from nightmares and an overwhelming sense of guilt and regret. But the way she kissed him back seemed to challenge that idea. What if *he* was what she wanted? Should he still pull away—for her own good? She didn't really know what she was getting into with him.

He sighed heavily as he rubbed the back of his neck again. Maybe he could come up with some answers when he'd rested and was able to sort out what was the best thing to do.

"The men haven't seen hide nor hair of Crowley," Levi said when he and Blane entered the kitchen from the mudroom. "But I can't help but think this is the calm before the storm."

Bone tired, Sean nodded. "You can be sure

he's not finished trying to get to Bailey—or me, for that matter." Sitting down, he motioned toward the coffeemaker. "Get a cup of coffee. I have a couple of ideas I need to run by the two of you about where we go from here. Then I'm going to try to get some shut-eye."

EIGHT

Bailey woke up with a start. It was still dark outside and the house was eerily quiet. Too quiet. There wasn't even the sound of a ticking clock. Maybe it was a case of nerves, but something just didn't feel right.

As her eyes became accustomed to the dark, she noticed the door to her temporary room open and a tall, broad-shouldered man slip inside. Her heart began to race, and fear froze her in place until she realized who it was.

"Sean?" she whispered, sitting up. "Is there a reason you're skulking around in the dark?"

When he walked over and sat on the bed beside her, he took her hand in his. "Crowley or one of his partners has breached the line of security."

Her breath caught. "He's in the house?"

"No, but he's on the property. Levi and

Blane are stationed at the front and back doors and if he gets past them, he'll have to go through me before he gets to you."

After throwing back the covers, she got up and walked over to get her borrowed boots. "One thing about going to sleep with my clothes on—it only takes a minute for me to be ready to flee for my life again."

"Sorry. I didn't have room to pack more than a change of clothes for you," he apologized as he eased over to the door to listen for any indication that someone had made it into the house.

When she sat on the bench at the end of the bed to put on the boots, she automatically made sure that her coat and scarf were within reach and her mittens and hat were in the pockets. She briefly wondered if from now on she would make a practice of having her things close by and ready to go. "I assume we won't be staying here for long. Did you and your brothers work out what we're going to do next?"

Instead of answering, he suddenly crossed over to the window to pull the curtain aside and look out into the backyard. "Something's going on outside and Levi and Blane are going out to see about it. They've apparently caught someone."

"Did they catch Crowley?" she asked anxiously, joining him at the window. She was tired of running and desperately wanted not to have to fear for her life anymore.

"I can't tell—but it looks like there's someone else approaching the back door. He's not one of my brothers and I don't like the way he's staying in the shadows. Stay here and lock the door behind me. Don't open it for anyone but me or one of my brothers."

When Sean slipped out the door, she locked it and then walked back to the window to see Blane and Levi, along with some of the ranch cowboys, escort the man they'd taken into custody into the barn closest to the house. That was one less man trying to kill her, but was it Crowley? And if not, where was the man—and how many cohorts did he still have out there? She had no doubt there were more than two of them.

An odd sound caught her attention and she looked over to see the doorknob turn slightly until it was stopped by the lock. "Sean?"

"Yeah."

The voice was muffled and didn't sound like Sean's, but it didn't sound like Crowley's deep growl, either. That was one voice she'd never as long as she lived forget and wouldn't mind never hearing again. Still, she couldn't be sure it wasn't one of the men working with Crowley. Sean would want her to be smart, to be cautious.

"Sean, what's going on out there? Who did your brothers catch?" she asked. If she could get him talking, she would know for sure if it was really Sean or someone trying to trick her. But instead of answering her in words, the man on the other side of the door groaned, low and pained.

Bailey's heart seized. If that really was Sean...if he was hurt, would she ever forgive herself if she kept the door barred against him? What if he needed her? It was worth the risk, she decided as she went to open the door for him.

To her shock and horror, Harold Crowley was standing on the other side with a thick cap in his hand that he had apparently used to disguise his voice. Fear sliced through her. Why had she opened the door? Sean had told her not to and she'd done it, anyway.

Smiling, Crowley stuck his gun in her face. "Surprise! I'll bet you didn't expect to see me here, did you, little sister?"

"Where's Sean?" she asked, not liking the fact that she hadn't heard a struggle from the kitchen or him shouting a warning for her to hide. Sean wouldn't have left the house— not when he had placed himself on guard to stop anyone from getting to her. If Crowley had gotten to her, it meant he would have gone through Sean first. "What have you done to him?"

"He's stretched out on the kitchen floor," Crowley said, sneering at her.

"You didn't…" She couldn't finish putting into words her worst fear.

"No, your boyfriend is still alive for the time being. Didn't think to pick up a silencer, and firing off a shot would bring those brothers of his running. We're going to do this nice and quiet—at least for now." He gave her a pointed look. "I'll come back later, after I've taken care of you, and finish him off. Now, come on. We need to get out of here before he wakes up."

"What did you do?" she demanded. If he was unconscious that meant Crowley had knocked him out.

"Let's just say he's taking a short nap for right now." He waved his gun at her coat and scarf. "Put those on."

He was standing between her and the door and with no other escape—other than the window, which she wouldn't be able to get open before he grabbed her—she had to keep stalling. One of Sean's brothers would surely come back inside soon. "I didn't hear a struggle. What did you do to him?"

"Not even the mighty Sean Hanson can fight off the effects of a stun gun and a hypodermic needle with a knockout drug in it." He picked up her coat and threw it at her. "Now, put this on or I'll shoot you right here and now."

"You said yourself— a gunshot will send everyone running right here. And then it would be back to jail for you—with even more crimes added to the list. All of this effort to get rid of a witness would be ruined just like that if you were caught with a gun in your hand and my body on the floor." She could see that he was getting steadily angrier and knew she was taking a huge chance that he'd lose his patience and carry out his threat, but she had to buy more time for someone to show up to help her and Sean. She didn't know what else to do.

"Shut up and put your coat on!" he barked, his wild-eyed gaze darting from her to the door.

Slowly putting her arms into the sleeves, she watched him and prayed. *Lord, please compel Sean's brothers to come back to the house.* Harold Crowley was desperate to get her and disappear into the darkness outside. Physically, she wasn't strong enough to stop him. Even if she put up a fight, he could easily overwhelm her. He might even have more knockout drugs on him.

And if he got her far enough away from the house, he would kill her. She had to keep that from happening. "You know you won't get away," she tried. "The Hanson brothers know every inch of this land. It won't take long before they realize I'm gone, realize what you did to Sean. You think they'll let you get away with hurting their big brother? They'll find you and when they do…"

"Shut! Up! And get moving."

She took her time wrapping her scarf around her neck and taking care to put on the mittens she'd borrowed and the hat Sean had given her to wear. Where were his brothers and why hadn't they come back inside?

Bailey jumped when Crowley grabbed her arm and jerked her toward the door. "You've dragged your feet long enough. Move!"

"How much do you trust your henchmen?" she asked, hoping that was a weak point she could exploit. "I'm sure whoever Sean's brothers are holding in the barn will tell them everything they need to know about where they can find you."

As Crowley shoved her down the hall toward the front door, he took hold of her scarf as he pushed her forward. "My friend in the barn knows better than to talk and you can thank that old man at the bank for sealing your fate," he said tightly. "If he hadn't ripped off my mask, I wouldn't have to kill you."

"You *don't* have to kill me," she argued. "I saw you rob the bank—so what? You were arrested coming out of that bank with a gun and the money. They don't need me to identify you. Not when they already know you're the guy responsible. Getting rid of me doesn't fix anything for you—it just adds more charges to the list, and more chances for you to get caught. You could let me go. You could run. You could go live your life somewhere other than here. No one's forcing you to follow through on this insane vendetta. You *don't have to do this*."

He held on to the scarf even as he shoved her through the front doorway and onto the porch. The scarf around her neck tightened painfully, causing her to cough and gag.

"Yes, I do." He pushed her down the steps and when she started to fall, he pulled the scarf even tighter, cutting off her ability to breathe but keeping her on her feet. "Now, shut up or I'm going to find something to stuff in your mouth until I get you somewhere I can silence you for good."

"Stop right there, Crowley!" Levi shouted from behind them. "You don't treat a woman that way. Turn her loose!" Apparently, he had reentered the house by way of the back door and heard the commotion on the front porch.

Thank You, Lord, for sending someone.

Crowley spun her around to put her between himself and Levi. For whatever reason, though, he seemed to change his mind about using her for a shield. Instead, he shoved her hard, turned and ran off into the darkness. Stumbling forward, she would have fallen on her face if not for Levi hurriedly catching her, then stepping around her, to run after Harold Crowley. When she looked up she saw what had apparently caused Crowley to decide to cut his losses and run. Blane was supporting Sean as they came across the wide porch and down the steps.

When he held out his free arm, she didn't think twice about closing the distance between them to step into Sean's embrace.

* * *

Sean held Bailey to him as Blane followed Levi in his pursuit of Harold Crowley. When he'd seen the man holding a gun on her and then pulling the scarf so tight that she choked, he thought he would come unglued. The adrenaline that had surged through his body helped to clear out some of whatever drug Crowley had injected into his arm, but his muscles and balance were still having a hard time trying to catch up.

Burying his face in her silky copper hair, he breathed in the scent of her herbal shampoo. "Are you all right?"

"I am now," she said, wrapping her arms around his waist and laying her head against his chest. "What happened to you? What did Crowley do?"

"I had just entered the kitchen when he came in from the mudroom." He shook his head. "He hit me with the stun gun almost before I realized it was him." He turned them to start up the steps. He wasn't sure how much longer his legs would support him, and falling on his face in the snow in front of her wasn't the kind of impression he wanted to make. "Let's go inside and sit down. We can start trying to figure this out in there."

With her help, he managed to navigate the porch steps to get inside. Once they were in the great room, he sank down on the heavy leather couch, pulling her down to sit beside him. "Are you sure you're all right? I saw him choking you with your scarf."

"It hurt when he was pulling it tight, but I don't think there's any real injury. I'm able to breathe and swallow without any problems," she said, unwinding the crocheted wrap and taking her coat off. "Now I'm just angry that I wasn't able to slow him down enough for your brothers to apprehend."

The moment she revealed the damage Crowley had caused—the bands of angry, reddish-purple marring her tender skin— the urge to go after the career criminal became a fire in his belly that wasn't going to go away anytime soon. It was one thing to Taser and drug him, but treating a vulnerable woman the way he'd done with Bailey was totally indefensible.

Gently touching the ugly marks on her throat with his fingertips, Sean shook his head. "If I have anything to do with it, he'll never touch you again."

The front door suddenly opened and Blane and Levi entered the great room. With just a glance, he could tell his brothers weren't happy. "Crowley must have had someone waiting for him close by," Levi said, taking off his coat and sitting down on the raised hearth of the river-rock fireplace. "We tracked him into the woods, but lost any sign of him about a quarter of a mile from the main road."

"And we heard a car pull out from close by," Blane added. "But all we could see were taillights as they raced away."

"Who was caught out by the barn?" Sean asked, wondering if it was the leak from the Cheyenne field office.

"We don't know," Blane answered as he sank into the armchair at the end of the couch. "We've never seen him before and he clammed up and won't talk to any of us."

"I took a picture of him to see if you know who he is," Levi added, taking his phone from his jeans pocket. He brought the picture up on the cell phone's screen and handed it to Sean. "Have you ever seen him before?"

"Can't say that I have." Sean shook his head. "He's probably someone Crowley met in prison."

"I know him," Bailey said, drawing a look of astonishment from him and his brothers. "That's Tom Miller. He comes into the bank all the time. He's married to my coworker Mary Ann." Sean watched her eyes widen as realization set in. "Mary Ann practically begged me to switch my lunch break with her the day the bank was robbed. She knew what was going to happen, didn't she?"

"I think that's a safe assumption." Sean gave her delicate hand a gentle squeeze.

"I can't believe Tom and Mary Ann are a part of this. They are both so nice and they have two of the cutest little boys." Bailey shook her head. "He teaches driver's ed and boys' gym classes at the high school, and Mary Ann is up for a promotion to loan officer at the bank. It just doesn't make sense that they would be criminals." She looked at the picture of Tom Miller again. "They have been so welcoming and helpful since I moved to Eagle Fork. How could they knowingly throw me into the middle of a bank robbery?"

Sean's stomach twisted into a knot at her obvious hurt feelings. A betrayal of trust could be a harsh reality.

"Maybe they've been having money problems," Blane said, settling back in the armchair. "Or they could have been tricked or blackmailed into going along with it. I know that doesn't make it right, but it might be an explanation, if not an excuse."

"Yeah, desperate people do desperate things," Levi added.

Sean put his arm around her shoulders. "It's usually best not to jump to conclusions until we have all the facts."

He didn't have all the pieces to the puzzle just yet. Priority one was to find out who Crowley had helping him at the Cheyenne field office. Also, he wanted to dig into what leverage Crowley had over Tom and Mary Ann Miller. Whatever it was, it caused two seemingly law-abiding citizens to risk their good standing in the community and turn into a bank robber's accomplices.

"Did you get hold of Agent Fowler?" Bailey asked.

"Not yet." He had intended to call Sam, but that all changed when Crowley showed up and he ended up taking an unplanned nap on the kitchen floor. "I'll call him as soon as I get another cup or two of coffee in me and hopefully chase away the rest of the brain fog left over by that drug."

"I'll go start another pot of coffee," Blane said, rising to his feet. "It's getting close to daylight, anyway."

Levi yawned and stretched before he got

up. "I think I'll whip up some bacon and eggs. How do you like your eggs, Bailey?"

"Over easy would be great," she said, smiling.

Levi grinned. "Scrambled it is."

Leaning toward her, Sean confided, laughing, "He only knows one way to cook eggs." As his brother walked by the couch, he asked, "Hey, what did you do with Miller?" They hadn't mentioned where they were holding him until Sam could get there.

"He's locked in the feed room in the barn with two men stationed by the door." Levi shook his head as he started toward the hall leading to the kitchen. "He wasn't talking but he looked mighty upset. I'd say this is the first time he's ever done something illegal or at least been caught at it."

Sean nodded. "All it takes is one bad decision to ruin a man's life."

"They both have so much to lose," Bailey said, her voice filled with sadness. "Do you think the authorities will go easy on them?"

"Here you go, big brother," Blane said, handing him a cup of coffee. "How do you take your coffee, Bailey? As soon as the smoke detector goes off, Levi will have breakfast ready and I'll have your coffee waiting for you at the table."

"I heard that!" Levi yelled from the kitchen.

She laughed. "I like my coffee black. Thank you."

"That's easy enough." Blane winked. "Even I can't mess that up."

"Thanks," Sean added, taking a sip from his mug.

He waited for his brother to go back to the kitchen to pour Bailey's coffee before he answered her question. "A lot of what happens will depend on the Millers' willingness to cooperate in building a case against Crowley and the circumstances surrounding their involvement. I don't know anything about them, but if this is their first offense and they are willing to help put Crowley behind bars for the rest of his life, they could end up with a much lighter sentence, possibly even probation with no time served. It just depends on what the prosecutor and their attorney work out and what the judge will go along with."

He watched her catch her lower lip between her teeth a moment before she nodded. "I'm just thinking about their little boys. They're only two and four and they need their parents."

He could only nod. His thoughts had automatically turned to the first woman the man had killed, the mother of two toddlers who were robbed of their mother's place in their lives. His stomach still clenched, and probably always would, whenever he thought about what had happened and how powerless he had been to stop it.

Needing to concentrate on the present and how he was going to save Bailey from the same fate, he cleared his throat. "My brothers and I had a long talk between the time you went to sleep and Crowley showed up and we decided that it would be best if you and I shelter in place until he's taken into custody."

"We're going to be staying here at Levi's?" Bailey wasn't sure what she expected, but she wasn't naive enough to think they had a lot of options. Sean had brought her to his ranch because the FBI safe houses weren't secure. A mountaintop cabin with limited access should have been the perfect solution, but no one had counted on the rogue agent using one of the government tracking gadgets to find their whereabouts on the mountain.

"Yes and no," he answered, taking a drink of his coffee. "Yes, we'll be here on the ranch, but not always in the same place.

We'll leave here and go home with Blane this morning and Thad will come over tonight to help with security. Then tomorrow morning we'll go home with Thad, and Levi will come over to his place tomorrow night for security detail. We all have enough hired men to throw up perimeters around the houses and barns so the level of security will always be top notch."

"But if that awful man is watching, won't he see us going from place to place?" She wasn't going to miss having to run for their lives, but she didn't understand how they would be all that much safer when the man could watch and follow them wherever they went.

"I'll let you in on a secret," he confided with a smile. "The Hanson brothers love their quad cab trucks. They're big, with roomy backseats, and we all have big attached garages with entrances straight into the house. We'll wait until daylight, lie down in the backseat of Blane's truck while it's still in Levi's garage and it will look like Blane is alone when he goes home. When we get to Blane's we'll wait until he pulls into his garage and closes the door before we get out."

Nodding, she began to understand his reasoning. "You want Crowley to see that Blane is alone, when he really isn't."

"Exactly. He'll think that we are still at Levi's." He took another drink of his coffee. "We'll have a couple of blankets over us and remain as still as possible for the ride over to Blane's part of the ranch. That way even if someone is watching from a distance with a scope on a high-powered rifle, they won't know for sure that we're in the truck."

"Won't they find the blankets suspicious?" she asked doubtfully.

He shook his head. "Not really. You're living in a state now where winters can be harsh and being stuck in a snowdrift is always a possibility. Most people have winter emergency provisions in their cars and trucks in case they become stranded and that includes blankets and quilts to stay warm."

"It sounds like a fairly good plan," she said, hesitantly. "But I hate for your brothers to be involved with something like this. They could get hurt."

"My brothers took great exception to Crowley threatening us, vandalizing the ranch and attacking me—multiple times." He rose to his feet and held out his hand to help her up from the couch. "Crowley made it personal. Now he has all of us to deal with."

"I just want all of you to be careful."

He stopped halfway across the great room and cupped her cheeks with his calloused palms. "I promise that we'll be as careful as we possibly can."

"You'd better be," she said, her voice catching at the thought of something happening to any of the brothers, but especially Sean. As she stared up into his warm brown gaze, her heart skipped a beat and she briefly wondered if he was going to kiss her again. She certainly wouldn't stop him if he did. But as the moment continued, she realized it probably wouldn't be a good idea. She was already scared senseless that something would happen to him or one of his brothers and she didn't want to be the distraction that caused it.

Feeling the need to lighten the mood before she did something stupid like break down and let her emotions have their soggy way, she took a deep breath. "You do know that the Hanson brothers aren't the only men who love trucks, right?"

He paused for a moment before he smiled. "Do tell."

"I grew up in a pretty rural area with lots

of agriculture and farming." She grinned. "I discovered a long time ago that men in rural areas love their trucks almost as much as their wives and girlfriends—sometimes more so."

"Well, I wouldn't go that far," he said, his deep chuckle sending a shiver down her spine.

As they walked into the kitchen, Bailey noticed they had been joined by another man—this one, she was sure, had to be Thad Hanson, the youngest of the brothers. The strong resemblance among the four men was absolutely remarkable. They all had different shades of brown hair, but they shared the same stunningly warm brown eyes, square jaw, laugh lines bracketing their mouths, and every one of them was over six feet tall.

"Hi. Nice to meet you." He stepped forward and stuck out his hand. "I'm Thad Hanson and you must be Bailey."

"It's nice to meet you, too, Thad." Her hand felt dwarfed by his. She'd always known she was petite, but standing next to the Hanson brothers, she felt as if she was amidst giants.

As she listened to the men discuss the plans Sean had explained to her a few minutes earlier, she was reminded again of how much she missed having a family. But more than that, she missed a family she'd never had—one that was at ease with each other, relaxed and joking and affectionate. Her parents had never been that way, even when her father was alive. Her mother had always been too preoccupied with treating Bailey as if she was made of eggshells and her father had gone along with her mother most of the time, just to keep the peace.

The love she saw among the men as they talked and made good-natured comments at each other's expense caused her to fight back tears. One day she was going to have a family like this one and she refused to let some lowlife like Harold Crowley take that away from her.

"Breakfast is just about ready," Levi said, interrupting her thoughts.

"Did you hear that?" Blane asked, tilting his head to one side. "I think the smoke detector is going off."

"Keep it up, little brother." Levi placed a heaping bowl of scrambled eggs on the table, along with a big platter of crispy bacon. "Don't think I won't get even with you one of these days when you least expect it."

The men all laughed as they took a seat at the big, round oak table and when Bailey took Sean's hand to her left, Levi reached for her hand from the right. She was heartened to see that holding hands around the table and bowing their heads to say grace seemed to come as naturally as breathing for the men.

They looked to her to lead the blessing, which she was happy to do. "Dear Lord, please bless this food we are about to eat, guide us throughout the day and please keep us safe from harm. In Your heavenly name, Amen."

When the prayer ended they all seemed to want to pass her something to put on her plate. "Ladies first," Levi said, handing her the bowl of scrambled eggs."

She'd no sooner passed the bowl on to Sean when Blane gave Levi the platter of bacon to send to her, followed by a plate of fluffy biscuits from Thad. Then a bowl filled with delicious-smelling, white country gravy was handed to her by Sean to fill the last open spot on her plate.

She waited until the men filled their plates before she took a bite of her eggs and bacon. "You're a good cook, Levi. This is delicious."

"You'll give him a big head, just because he's showed off the only thing he knows how to cook." Blane groaned and shook his head. "Now there'll be no living with him."

As Sean and his brothers continued eating, their easy banter gradually turned more serious. "When you call Agent Fowler are you going to let him know your plans on evading Crowley?" she asked.

"I'm not sure I'd feel comfortable telling him over an unsecure line." Sean shrugged. "I don't know if the phone lincs in the field office have been tapped or if someone is monitoring Sam's cell phone."

"It might be wise just to tell him you'll be staying here at the ranch and leave it at that," Thad suggested.

"That's what I'm thinking," Sean agreed.

"Are we waiting until Agent Fowler comes to take Tom Miller into custody before we leave to go to Blane's?" she asked.

He stood up and took his and her empty plates to the sink. "If I talk to him in person that would prevent anyone from monitoring the call."

Listening to the brothers reasoning made her feel even more confident that these men could and would keep her safe, just as if she was part of their family. Her heart stalled at the thought and she did her best to ignore the overwhelming sense of longing that filled her. Was she so desperate to be part of a family that she latched on to the first one she became acquainted with?

Unsettled, she decided she needed a little alone time to sort through her tangled thoughts and emotions. "If you'll excuse me, I think I'll go to the guest room to straighten up and make the bed before Agent Fowler arrives."

"No problem. Take all the time you need," Sean said, giving her a smile that warmed her heart. "Sam is probably going to want to ask you some questions about the Millers. I'll let you know when he gets here."

She nodded, then turning to the rest of the men, said, "Breakfast was amazing and I really got a kick out of the bickering. Thank you all for being a bright spot in an otherwise stressful situation."

Before she could do something stupid like admit how much she longed to be part of a family like theirs, she fled to the guest room.

NINE

Sean was surprised when Sam showed up with a couple of US Marshals to arrest Tom Miller, instead of relying on the Wyoming Highway Patrol. Earlier, the man hadn't been sure if the mole was within the Bureau's ranks or the Marshal Service. Had that changed? Did Sam know who it was now?

"Any idea who's leaking information to Crowley?" he asked.

His friend shook his head. "The only thing I'm sure of is the marshals are clean. The leak is definitely within the Bureau."

"I hate to hear that." He didn't like learning about misconduct in any law enforcement agency, but it was a deeper disappointment to hear it was inside an institution he had proudly served for seven years.

Sam ran an agitated hand through his

dark blond hair. "Believe me, I feel the same way."

"What are you going to do about Miller's wife, Mary Ann?" Sean asked, watching the two US Marshals lead the woman's clearly defeated husband to a federal transport van.

"I've already sent a couple of marshals to pick her up, but I need to talk to Ms. O'Keefe and determine exactly what took place when Mrs. Miller asked to switch lunch hours." Sam yawned. "I'll also need to question the bank manager to see if he had to approve the swap."

Sean could see the dark circles under his friend's eyes and knew Sam was as sleep deprived as he was. "Not getting much sleep these days?"

Sam smiled tiredly and shook his head. "I haven't slept for more than a couple of hours at a stretch for the past four days."

"I don't know about you, but I'm getting too old for this much sleep deprivation," Sean said as they walked toward Levi's back porch.

His friend nodded. "Yeah, I'll be forty next month and every year it gets harder and harder to live on coffee and energy drinks during an active case."

"Yeah, I remember those days." They were silent as they climbed the back steps.

"Let me ask you something, Sean. Do you ever miss the job?" Sam asked, taking him by surprise.

Sean shook his head. "Not in the least. Over the past three years I've learned that I'm much happier enjoying the peace and quiet of nature as opposed to the stress of having to make life or death decisions in a split second." He still had nightmares from his seven years at the Bureau and had been glad that he wasn't adding more.

When they entered the kitchen, they were greeted by Levi and Blane sitting at the table going over plans to add a new herd of cattle to Thad's part of the ranch. "Have a seat," Levi said. "You look as tired as we all feel."

"How do you take your coffee, Agent Fowler?" Blane asked, standing to reach up in the cabinet for a mug.

"Black with sugar." Sam looked grateful when Blane put a large cup of coffee, a spoon and the sugar bowl in front of him. "This is all that's keeping me going. Thanks."

Before Sean could excuse himself to go get Bailey, she walked into the kitchen, looking amazing with her long, straight, copper hair framing her sweet face. He swallowed hard and forced himself to abandon that train of thought. All he'd been able to think about after he'd kissed her had been how he wanted to kiss her again. He'd even been so preoccupied with it that he'd let down his guard and Bailey had come close to becoming one of Crowley's victims. He had to make sure that didn't happen again.He had enough on his plate without thinking of things that were counterproductive to his sanity and her safety.

When she walked over to the table, she directed her gaze at Sam. "Hello, Agent Fowler."

Sam nodded. "Ms. O'Keefe."

As the men remembered their manners and started to rise from their chairs at the table, she shook her head. "No need to get up."

Sean ignored her and stood up to hold her chair, then sat in the one next to her. "Doing okay?" he whispered while Sam took Levi and Blane's statements about catching Miller the night before.

She nodded. "I saw the US Marshals leading Tom away. What's going to happen to him now?"

"He'll be interrogated and most likely arraigned and charged within a day or two.

After that, if he has a good lawyer, he might be able to get bail if he isn't deemed a flight risk." He shrugged. "If they think he'll try to run or can't afford bail, he'll sit in jail until his trial."

"What about Mary Ann?" she asked.

"She's being picked up now for Sam to question as soon as he gets back to the office in Cheyenne." He decided not to tell her that the woman would most likely be arrested and held over for arraignment for her part in the crime. He knew that would be upsetting for Bailey, not just about Mary Ann Miller's involvement in the crime, but because of the two little boys who would be without their mother and father, at least for a while.

Sam finished up Blane and Levi's statements, and the two headed out to handle some of the ranch chores.

As his brothers left the house, Sean turned to Sam. "Do you have any idea who put the GPS bug on Bailey's coat?"

Sam shook his head. "Not yet. But whoever he is, if he's been using our resources to track your whereabouts, I'll find out. And when I do find out, we'll have uncovered the identity of the office leak." Turning to Bailey, he flipped to a blank page in his small notepad. "What can you tell me about the morning of the robbery? Was there anything that your coworker Mary Ann Miller said or did that was unusual? Did she seem anxious or upset in any way?"

"The only thing that was odd about that day was her wanting to switch lunch breaks." Bailey frowned. "She had asked me when I first started working at the bank, if I would mind permanently taking the later lunch because she used her lunchtime to pick up her oldest son from the babysitter to take him to afternoon preschool. I understood and told her I would be more than happy to have the later lunch. But the day of the robbery, she told me she had an important errand she needed to run and asked if I could switch with her and take the earlier break."

"Did she indicate what kind of errand it was or where she'd be going?" he asked.

When she stared off into space as if trying to recall something, Sean reached over and covered her hand with his. "Anything you remember could help the investigation, Bailey."

"I don't know if this has anything to do with the case or not, but Mary Ann mentioned something about needing to go home and pack a bag for the boys, then take them to her mother's so that she and Tom could take a trip together over the weekend. Since the robbery was on Friday..."

"It's a safe assumption they were planning to meet up with Crowley somewhere," Sam said, nodding as he jotted down notes on the pad of paper. "Did she happen to mention a destination?"

Bailey shook her head. "No, but she said she was really excited about spending time alone with her husband for the first time since their oldest child was born." Bailey frowned. "But come to think of it, she looked and acted more uneasy than excited."

"Anything else?" Sam asked.

"No. We didn't really have much time to talk. We had a steady stream of bank customers most of the morning and by the time it slowed down, it was time for me to go to lunch." She sighed. "When I got back at noon, Mary Ann left to take her break and five minutes later Harold Crowley entered the bank."

Sean had no doubts that both of the Millers were in on the heist, but how did a couple in their late twenties with no prior history of criminal activities know someone like Crowley? Where was the connection? And what linked them all with someone in the FBI Cheyenne field office?

When Blane parked in his garage at his house and closed the overhead door, Sean flipped back the colorful quilt that was covering them, and Bailey sat up in the backseat of the truck. They'd waited to make their move until Agent Fowler left the ranch to go back to Cheyenne to interrogate Mary Ann. Bailey still couldn't believe that she was involved in the crime. She just couldn't imagine anyone doing anything to jeopardize their family, their jobs and the life they had built for themselves in a nice little community like Eagle Fork.

"I think that worked out pretty well." Sean opened the back driver's side door, got out and set his backpack on the concrete garage floor.

Wondering if they had really gotten away with the ruse, she smiled when he reached to lift her down from the truck. "Well, it was interesting and if the running commentary from your brother is correct, it appears we weren't followed."

"That was the plan." He stared at her for what seemed like an eternity, and just when she thought he was going to kiss her again, he cleared his throat and stepped back. Placing his hand to the small of her back, he guided her toward the door into the house.

Taking a deep breath, she tried not to be disappointed. He'd only kissed her once, but it had left a lasting impression on her and she wouldn't have minded if he'd kissed her again. And that was the problem. She was starting to have more complex feelings for him, feelings that she wasn't sure he returned. She wanted to believe that the kiss meant something—that *she* meant something to him beyond just being a woman he was guarding. But how could she be sure? She had zero experience with men, not because she was closed off to having a relationship, but because none of the boys she knew in school wanted to have anything to do with the class oddball. That had followed her through college and by the time she graduated, she had to take care of her mother and wouldn't have had time for a relationship, anyway. Besides, Sean hadn't talked about the kiss, hadn't made any move to repeat it. Maybe he'd just gotten caught up in the moment. She wished she knew, one way or the other, but she didn't feel brave enough to bring it up.

"What time will Thad be here this evening?" she asked in an effort to get her mind off her romantic uncertainties.

"I'm not sure," he answered, frowning. "Why?"

She shrugged one shoulder. "I was thinking you all have disrupted your routines in order to keep me alive, the least I can do is cook dinner for you."

His frown turned into an easy smile. "That's nice of you, but you really don't have to do that."

"I'd really like to have something to do to keep my mind off everything," she admitted as he walked her through the kitchen and great room. "And I do want to show you how grateful I am."

He stopped and turned to face her. "Bailey, what my brothers and I are doing is nothing more than what's right. But if you want to cook a meal for us, we'll appreciate it." His low chuckle sent a shiver right through her a moment before he kissed her forehead. "Anything you make will be better than the can of soup or box of macaroni and cheese Blane will set in front of us if you don't step in."

Suddenly feeling like air was in short supply, she forced a smile, hoping it looked casual and relaxed. "Happy to help. And I'll do the same thing tomorrow evening when Levi comes over to Thad's."

"You're incredible," he said, giving her a smile that caused a hitch in her breathing.

She felt her cheeks grow warm from his compliment as she followed him down the hall to a door she assumed to be the guest room. "I, uh, don't know about being incredible," she stammered. "But I would feel guilty about sentencing you to a meal out of a can or a box."

When he opened the door to a beautiful bedroom with a big log bed covered by a colorful, patchwork quilt, her breath caught. "This is perfect. Did Blane do the decorating?"

Scan threw back his head and laughed so hard tears filled his eyes. "That's about the funniest thing I've heard in a month of Sundays. Our mom decorated for him and you should be glad she did. Blane's idea of decorating would be a sleeping bag or a camp cot and a lawn chair for a bedside table."

"Oh my." Before Bailey could stop herself she laughed just as hard as Sean. "We shouldn't mock. Maybe Blane is just a minimalist."

"That's one way of putting it," Sean said, wiping his eyes. Turning, he walked over to the door. "There are towels in the linen cabinet in the bathroom, as well as shampoo, shower gel and just about anything else you might need."

"Compliments of your mother?" she asked, grinning.

Grinning back at her, he nodded. "It certainly wasn't something Blane thought to stock."

"Don't forget to call Thad and tell him to be here at six for dinner this evening," she said as he walked out into the hall.

"He'll be grateful for a decent meal." Sean started to close the door, then turned back, smiling. "He's no better at cooking than Blane is."

When the door clicked shut behind him, Bailey sat down on the side of the bed and blindly stared at the varnished log walls while she tried to reason with herself. She wasn't used to all the affection or praise that Sean showered on her—and that had her conflicted over what it might mean. Maybe this was normal for him? How could she tell if she was special? She was in uncharted waters here, and couldn't be sure if she was misreading the signals completely. She didn't know what he was feeling—and she wasn't even sure she could trust her own heart. Wasn't there some kind of syndrome where people thought they had developed feelings for someone who saved them? Maybe when this was over, her feelings would fade away.

But one thing she knew for sure was that when it was over and Harold Crowley was caught, their lives would go back to normal. That meant she'd go back to her solitary life—and Sean wouldn't be in it anymore.

Sean walked into the kitchen to find Bailey peeling tomatoes and cutting them into cubes to add to a saucepan on the electric range. "Where did you get the fresh tomatoes?" he asked, going over to the sink to wash his hands. If she was going to cook supper for him and two of his brothers, the least he could do was help her.

"I gave Blane a grocery list and he went into Eagle Fork to get the ingredients for Swiss Steak, garlic-and-herb mashed potatoes and Southern-style green beans." She held up a hand as if she expected him to be angry. "And before you go ballistic because Blane left me alone while you were asleep, he made me promise to lock myself in the guest room while he was gone. Which I did. He also said that if I heard something that didn't seem right, I should knock on the wall between my room and yours and you would be up and ready to do battle immediately. But there weren't any attacks and you got some much-needed rest. So everything worked out fine and there's no need for you to go into macho mode." Her sweet smile effectively cooled any irritation he felt toward Blane and had him smiling helplessly back at her in return.

After four days on an adrenaline roller coaster, he'd been ready to drop in his tracks. Fortunately, he had more or less passed out and hadn't dreamed. It also didn't hurt to wake up and find Bailey happily bustling around in the kitchen.

"Okay, I'll let Blane off the hook…this time. By the way, where is he?"

She reached for a cutting board on the counter. "I think he said he was going out to the equipment barn to talk to his foreman about changing the tires on a wagon and tractor."

He glanced out the window to see his brother crossing the yard to the stables. "Is there anything I can do to help?" he asked, turning back to watch Bailey chop the bacon like a top chef.

"If you wouldn't mind watching the tomatoes for me, I'll finish chopping this fried bacon and get the green beans started cooking." He watched as she moved around the kitchen like a graceful little whirlwind, putting sliced green beans into a large saucepan with broth, adding crispy bacon bits, chopped onions and a small amount of bacon drippings before setting it onto a back burner to cook. "How is your arm?" she asked as she reached for the packages of steak.

"It's doing fine." He looked at the tomatoes and wondered what she meant about watching them. Watch them do what? "Should I stir these or something?"

"That would be great." She poured olive oil into a big skillet. "Is your arm sore? You know what Levi said. If it gets overly sore he'll talk to one of his doctor friends about a prescription for antibiotics."

"Actually, it feels pretty good." He stirred the tomatoes stewing in the saucepan as he watched her start searing pieces of steak. "Did your mother teach you to cook?"

She smiled fondly as she nodded. "She'd wanted a child for so long, she spent every possible moment doing things with me and teaching me all the things she knew how to do. I started helping her cook when I was so small I had to stand on a chair to reach the stove."

"She sounds like she was a wonderful mother. What was the first thing she taught you to make?" he asked, wanting to know more about her.

"Cookies."

"I like cookies," he said, grinning.

"Is that a hint?" When he nodded, she laughed. "You're as subtle as a sledgehammer."

When he stopped laughing, he shrugged. "I don't want you to think that I expect you to make cookies."

"I know you don't, but when I was poking around in Blane's cabinets to see what I needed from the grocery store, I discovered a jar of peanut butter and thought that peanut butter cookies with homemade hot chocolate in front of the fire after dinner might be nice."

"That sounds like a winner to me." He stirred the tomatoes again. "What else can I do, now that I've added cookies to the menu?"

"You can slice those two green bell peppers into thin strips and then cut the big red onion into rings. Once they're ready, separate the onion rings and add them and the pepper strips on top of the steaks, put the lid on the skillet and turn the burner down to medium low." She reached for the saucepan and poured the tomatoes on top of the steaks. "While you do that, I'll whip up some peanut butter cookie dough."

Working side by side in the kitchen with Bailey gave Sean a glimpse of the life he'd always thought he wanted. Now he knew for sure that it was what he wanted. But he also feared it was something he would never have. How could he justify saddling Bailey with his nightmares or the guilt he still harbored for the death of an innocent woman who had been counting on him to save her?

His stomach twisted and he had to remind himself to breathe. He glanced over at Bailey, watching her flatten balls of cookie dough with a fork before sliding the cookie sheet into the oven. When she turned and smiled at him, his heart thumped hard against his ribs, and his lungs couldn't seem to draw in enough air.

Taking a deep breath, he finished cutting the onion and peppers, added them to the skillet with the steak and washed his hands. "I'm going to step out onto the back porch and check with Blane about the number of men we'll have on the perimeter tonight."

"No problem." She smiled brightly. "Thank you for helping with dinner."

"I'll be back in time to set the table and help with anything else you need," he said, inching his way toward the door. If he didn't get out of there and quick, he wasn't sure he wouldn't do something like kiss her again.

When he escaped to the porch, he pulled in a big breath of cold air, allowing it to clear his head as he slowly exhaled. He needed to get his act together. At some later point he could figure out what to do about the yearnings that got stronger by the day. In the meantime, he would tend to the business of keeping Bailey alive. Then once she went back to her life in Eagle Fork, he'd figure out what came next—whether it would include trying for something more with Bailey...or retreating to the top of Cougar Mountain to take some pictures of the wildlife and do his best not to think about the rest of his life without her.

TEN

"Bailey, that was the best home cooked meal I've had since our mom and dad moved to Arizona," Blane said, leaning back in his chair at the table.

"I have to agree." Thad rubbed his flat stomach. "I don't think I could eat another thing."

"Are you sure you can't eat just a little more?" she asked, rising to clear the table. "I made peanut butter cookies and homemade hot chocolate. I was thinking we could have them while we sit around the fireplace and you all tell me stories about the antics of the Cougar Mountain Mavericks."

"Peanut butter cookies are my favorite and homemade hot chocolate is the best," Thad said, his grin wide. "The day I can't make room for either one of those is the day they bury me."

Sean stood up and shook his head. "Bailey, you worked hard and made us a fantastic meal. We'll take care of clearing the table and cleaning the kitchen." When he turned his gaze on his brothers, they both jumped to their feet and started taking bowls of leftovers off the table and gathering empty plates and silverware to load into the dishwasher.

As the men cleaned up the kitchen and stored leftovers in the refrigerator, she poured hot chocolate into mugs, put a scoop of marshmallow cream on top of each one and handed them to Sean and his brothers when they started toward the great room. "Let me carry the plate of cookies," Sean offered with a wink. "I can't run the risk of my brothers eating all the cookies before I get my share."

She laughed as she sat down on the couch. "I could always make you some more."

His warm gaze met hers. "Thank you again for making a delicious supper for us."

"I should be the one thanking you," she admitted. "I enjoy cooking, but I rarely get to cook for anyone. It's always more fun when I'm cooking for more than just myself."

He nodded. "I'm sure it is and believe me,

we really do appreciate you going to all the trouble."

"Bailey, the next time you want to cook and you don't have anyone in particular to feed, just say the word and I'll be there with bells on," Blane said, taking a bite out of a cookie. As she watched, he closed his eyes and smiled. "I think these are as good as Mom's and that's saying something."

"Come by my place and get me anytime you have food going to waste," Thad said, grinning. "I'll be more than happy to eat something I didn't have to cook."

The easy banter continued for some time and it was something that Bailey knew she would never get tired of. It was so much nicer listening to the brothers laugh and joke with each other than to sit in silence before, during and after every meal.

While Blane and Thad discussed the merits of a homemade cookie over the packaged kind, she turned to Sean. "You're awfully quiet. Is something wrong?"

He shook his head as he stretched and rested his arm along the back of the couch behind her. "Sam called this afternoon while I was outside talking to Blane. He said that Tom Miller still isn't talking, but he did ask for a lawyer and was assigned a public defender."

"What about Mary Ann?" She hated the thought of a mother being separated from her little boys—but if she refused to cooperate, Bailey was sure the authorities wouldn't let her go home.

"She isn't talking much, either, but Sam did find out that her sons are being cared for by her mother." He reached over to place his hand on top of hers. "And he said she asked if she could temporarily make her mother their legal guardian."

"I think that would be for the best." It was a huge relief to know that the toddlers would be in the care of someone who loved them. "Mary Ann told me that her mother and the boys are extremely close. That might make things a little easier for them if they have to be away from Mary Ann and Tom for any length of time."

He nodded. "I'm sure the authorities will make every effort to do what's in the boys' best interest."

"I hope so." She started to get up to carry the empty cookie plate to the kitchen, but when Sean, Blane and Thad's cell phones all beeped with an incoming text that made them all frown, she stopped short. "What's happened?"

"Levi's had a little trouble over at his place," Sean said, walking over to place his hands on her shoulders. "One of his men found a body in the barn."

"Oh my!" She covered her mouth with both hands. "Does Levi know...who..."

"We're going out to check in with the guys and see if everyone is accounted for here," Blane said, heading toward the kitchen with Thad right behind him.

When Sean pulled her into his arms, her heart stalled. It had to be someone she knew. Nothing else would explain the look of pained compassion on his face. "It was Mr. McKenzie, the bank security guard," he said, his voice low and compassionate.

"No-o-o..." Her knees threatened to buckle and she grabbed the front of Scan's shirt to keep from falling as tears ran down her cheeks. "Not Earl. He's...such a sweet... old gentleman."

He led her back to the couch and once she was seated, he sat down beside her and pulled her into his arms. "Levi is waiting on the county sheriff and the coroner to get there, but he said it looks like Mr. McKenzie was shot at point-blank range."

Rushing through her mind was a stream of good memories of the kind old man. He was one of the ushers at the church she started attending when she first moved to Eagle Fork, and right from the start Earl McKenzie and his wife, Mavis, had treated her like a granddaughter. She sat beside them through services and they always saved a place for her at their table when the church had potluck dinners. "Was he shot because of me?"

He shook his head as his arms tightened around her. "I don't know for certain, but I don't think so. I suspect it was because he saw Crowley's face during the robbery or at least Crowley thinks he did."

"He was only trying to protect me." Her heart broke at the thought of what Earl's wife of fifty years would go through when she learned she'd lost her beloved husband.

"Crowley has a habit of eliminating whoever has the misfortune to see him without his mask."

Bailey shook her head. "He can't kill everyone who saw his face. You and I saw him, all of the US Marshals and FBI who were there that day saw him. And unless the traitor in the FBI office erased it, there are security cameras that recorded everyone who entered the bank that day. He was wearing his mask at the start, but there must be footage of him without it, too." She stopped to look at him. "You don't think…"

"Probably," he said, nodding. "The reason Crowley has someone in the FBI he's working with, is to do things like erase surveillance footage, put GPS tracking devices in place to track his targets and give him advance warning of what the FBI has planned next."

"I just want all of this running and hiding to stop," she said, becoming more angry by the second. Usually, she didn't like being angry. But right now it felt good to release some of the tension gripping her. "I don't want any more death threats or any more innocent people losing their lives. I want Harold Crowley to be caught and held accountable for robbing and terrorizing people, for killing decent people like Earl." She trembled from the emotions coursing through her that she seemed to have no control over. "I'm tired. I want to go to bed at night and not expect to be awakened because someone is trying to catch and kill us." Tears began to course down her cheeks and she couldn't seem to stop them. "I…don't want to…be afraid anymore," she sobbed. "I… hate being…afraid."

* * *

Sean held her close as he tried to figure out a way to ease her fears. Her life had been threatened so many times in the past several days, he wasn't the least bit surprised she'd come to her breaking point. Truth to tell, he had expected it way before now.

The first time he'd heard her voice during the negotiation he'd imagined she was the soft, gentle type of woman, one who was likely to be intimidated easily. He couldn't have been more wrong. After observing her in so many stressful situations, his respect for her courage had grown tenfold.

She'd faced the threat of being shot at point-blank range during a robbery without falling apart, had made a blind run for it in knee-deep snow across the top of a mountain peak at night to hole up in a cave with two gunmen hot on their trail, had fallen off a cliff and almost plunged into a deep ravine. She'd been shot at, not just once but several times, had faced down a mountain lion and had managed to stall a ruthless killer until she evaded a kidnap attempt that nearly ended her life. It was no wonder her nerves had finally gotten the better of her. And yet, despite her tears now, he knew that she would come back from this even stronger. She had an iron will to survive and, although she had cracked under the pressure, she was far from broken.

"Bailey, you're a strong woman—actually the strongest woman I've ever met." He ran his hand up and down her back in a comforting manner. "I've met trained agents who couldn't face the threats you've dealt with the past six days."

"It seems…like I've done nothing…but cry," she said haltingly as she wiped her tears on the handkerchief he dug out of his back jeans pocket and handed to her.

"The only times you've cried have been because you feared for mine or my brothers' safety, because you were mourning the loss of your parents and now because of your totally understandable sadness over Earl McKenzie's passing," he said gently. "Until now I've never seen you give in to any kind of fear for your own well-being. After all you've been through, don't you realize how remarkable that is?"

She shrugged one shoulder. "I really never gave it a lot of thought." They were silent for several moments before she asked, "Will it…ever end? Will we ever be free of having to look over our shoulders?"

Hugging her to him, he tipped her chin

up with his index finger until his gaze captured hers. "Yes, it will end and yes, we'll be free from all the drama. Crowley will be caught and go to jail, we'll find out who the mole is in the Cheyenne office and he'll be incarcerated, as well."

"After my mother passed away, I wanted new experiences and exciting adventures," she murmured. "But this wasn't exactly what I had in mind."

Leaning back to look at her, he frowned. "What do you mean?"

She sighed and looked down at the floor. "I know my parents loved me more than life itself and I loved them every bit as much. And don't think I don't consider myself extremely blessed to have had them, because I do. I know there are kids out there who would do anything for even one parent who truly loves them unconditionally—much less two. But to say I led a sheltered life is an understatement." She stared down at her hands twisted into a tight knot in her lap. "My entire life I wasn't allowed to do things that other kids my age were doing because my mother was afraid I would get hurt or have some kind of health issue. When my dad was alive, it wasn't too bad. He would sometimes intervene and reason with my mother, and I was allowed to learn things like how to ride a bicycle and jump rope. But after he passed away when I was twelve, my mother became obsessive about my health and safety to the point where I felt smothered. Her usual caution became ten times stronger because she was afraid I might have inherited my father's heart defect. Even though some of the best pediatric heart specialists tested and retested me and assured her I was perfectly healthy, she wouldn't allow me to participate in sports or even play like other kids because she was afraid of what might happen to me."

"Every parent worries about their kids." He couldn't say his mother had been a helicopter parent, but he and his brothers gave her plenty of reason to worry and had most likely caused her to miss a lot of sleep.

Bailey surprised him when she shook her head vehemently. "You don't understand, Sean. My mother insisted that I couldn't take physical education in school. I wasn't allowed to go on field trips unless she was able to get the day off from work because something might happen to me. Can you imagine how much that set me apart from everyone else at my school? Take it from me, that practically paints a sign on your back saying 'weirdo,' which opens the door for a bully to step right into your life and make you miserable."

As he listened to her give him a glimpse into her childhood, he began to understand her insistence that she wasn't a "hothouse flower" and didn't need to be spared the stark details of their situation. Clearly, her mother's choices had left their marks on her in ways he never would have anticipated.

He respected where she was coming from but that didn't do a thing to tamp down the need for him to keep her safe and happy. He tried to tell himself that he would feel the same toward any woman, but he knew better. Bailey was the first woman he'd ever guarded who brought out that depth of protectiveness in him. It left him feeling weak in the knees, like he would move heaven and earth to be there for her.

He swallowed hard and tried to shake off the emotions coursing through him. He was a far cry from being anyone's rock and he had no business thinking along those lines.

"You were bullied in school?"

When she nodded, his gut clenched into a knot. "It wasn't really vicious, but I did feel like a freak sometimes." She sighed. "My mother told me that the ones who made fun of me were just doing that to make themselves feel less vulnerable. Now that I'm an adult, I know she was right. But that certainly didn't make me feel any better at the time, especially while I was all alone, sitting along the sidelines watching them play like I wasn't allowed to do. I always thought that if I had the opportunity, I'd get out there and participate, not just watch life pass me by."

"That's why you want adventure and excitement in your life?" he asked, his chest tightening just a bit. He'd been right about her being vivacious and full of life. Was that too much of a contrast with his own lifestyle, in the calm and quiet of Cougar Mountain?

"Sean, are you all right?" she asked, her expression filled with concern.

Taking her hand in his, he nodded. "I'm just trying to picture you as a quiet little girl sitting on the sidelines." He smiled. "That doesn't sound like the Bailey O'Keefe I've come to know." He wasn't about to tell her that he had been lamenting the fact that they were so different.

"More like squirmed and fidgeted the whole time I had to sit there and watch everyone else have fun." She laughed. "I look back on it now and wonder why on earth I didn't just get up and join them like most kids would have done. I could have hidden it from my mom if I'd really tried."

"I know exactly why you didn't." Sean tucked her hair behind her ear. "You were an obedient little girl who didn't want to break the rules your mother had set in place because you respected and loved her."

She gave him one of those smiles that never failed to make his heart race. "I think you're right. I was taught in Sunday school and at home to try very hard not to break rules or disobey because when my parents told me that I couldn't do something it was their way of saying they loved me and were trying to protect me."

"Yup, that's what my parents always told me and my brothers right before they grounded us for doing something we had been told not to do," he admitted, laughing.

Bailey laughed with him, just as he'd intended. "Your mother definitely had her hands full, didn't she?"

"Still does. Our dad always told us stories about the things he did as a boy and he'd end it with, 'If you try that, don't tell your mother. She'll think I put you up to it.'" He grinned. "He shouldn't have trusted us with such good ammunition. In an effort to get ourselves out of trouble, we always told her that Dad did it when he was a kid so it couldn't be that bad."

"Oh wow!" She looked wistful. "I'll bet she loved every minute of raising you boys. And your dad," she added, laughing.

Sean grinned. "Actually, I think she's still working on raising my dad."

When they fell silent, she sighed. "Thank you for distracting me from my pity party."

Frowning, he shook his head. "I don't know what you're talking about."

She gave him that look a woman gives a man when she thinks he's being deliberately obtuse. "I know you did that on purpose— telling stories about you and your brothers and your father's part in the mischief you got into to take my mind off losing Earl and how lonely I was as a child."

"You haven't had much to smile about the past several days," he said, knowing he'd do whatever he could to lift her spirits. He continued to gaze into her emerald eyes, fighting himself until he couldn't fight anymore.

Slowly lowering his head, he brushed her mouth with his at first, then finally settled his lips on hers. His heart took off like a racehorse when she circled his neck with her arms, leaned closer and kissed him back.

A warm feeling filled him and a sense of coming home settled within his soul. Holding her in his arms, feeling her heartbeat keep time with his own, seemed to make his world make sense again.

When he leaned back, she stared up at him and smiled. "Thank you for caring about...my smile."

He nodded, unable to think of a thing to say that wouldn't make him sound like an idiot. Instead of ruining the moment with the wrong words, he kissed her forehead, then stood up and held out his hand to help her up from the couch. "I should check in with Blane and Thad and find out how things are here on the south end of the mountain."

"Maybe since we gave the appearance of staying with Levi, there won't be any trouble here this evening," she said, picking up the cookie plate and a couple of mugs.

"Let's hope so." He picked up the two remaining mugs and walked into the kitchen with her.

"Looks like everything here is clear for now," Blane said, coming in with Thad from outside.

"Let's hope it stays that way," Sean commented a moment before the distinct sound of gunfire rang out and one of the kitchen windows shattered, spraying bits of glass all over the floor.

ELEVEN

Dropping the plate and mugs she held, Bailey covered her head with her hands and started to run for the hall, but Sean grabbed her at the waist and pivoted toward the kitchen island, pulling her down to the floor behind it. Once they were both safely behind the large wood-and-marble cabinet in the center of the kitchen, Sean drew his gun from the holster on his belt and held it at the ready.

Dear Lord, please keep all of us safe and make Harold Crowley and his men go away and leave us alone, she prayed fervently.

The sound of men shouting and guns being fired outside sent shivers of dread coursing through her. The very last thing she wanted was for anyone to get hurt or killed because of her. It was bad enough that dear old Earl had lost his life. When he'd charged at Crowley and inadvertently pulled down his mask, he'd just been trying to help her. He hadn't known that in the process, he was sealing his own fate. To have more men die trying to keep her alive was unthinkable.

When the lights went out, she wrapped her arms around her knees and tried to think of something she could do to stop the madness that had dominated her and Sean's world for the past week. Short of surrendering herself to Crowley in exchange for Sean and his brothers' safety, she couldn't think of a thing, and as naive as she was, even she knew that wouldn't work. He wouldn't be satisfied until he'd killed both of them, as well as killing anyone who got in his way.

"Thanks, Thad. Now that the lights are out, we've got a fighting chance," Blane said from the other end of the island as he quickly slid back the pump on the shotgun to load a shell into the chamber. Once it was ready, he pushed it forward into position along the barrel. She briefly wondered where he'd come up with the gun, then realized that the Hanson brothers had prepared for the possibility of an attack.

"Are you all right?" Sean asked, putting his free arm around her shoulders.

Nodding, she took a deep breath and lifted her head from her knees. "I'm trying to figure out what we have to do to dissuade this madman from his mission to kill us."

"You're amazing." Sean stared at her a moment before he hugged her to him, then let her go. "If you guys have the back covered, Bailey and I are going to take up position at the front of the house."

"We've got this," Thad assured them.

"Good idea. I'm going to call my foreman to check if they have any casualties and gauge what they can see from their positions in the outbuildings," Blane added.

"Sounds good. Let me know what you find out." Sean turned to her and motioned toward the hallway. "Crawl ahead of me. As soon as we reach the hall, I'll take the lead."

"Where are we going in the front of the house?" She started crawling across the kitchen.

"We're going to take up position behind the couch." When she stopped for him to go ahead of her, she followed him down the hall and across the great room to the couch. Reaching over the back, he removed a couple of the stuffed leather seat cushions and placed them close by. "If someone starts firing through the windows in here, I want you to wedge yourself between the floor and the couch and pull the cushions over you as best you can."

Her heartbeat sped up. Was this some kind of last stand?

"Sean, please be careful," she said, trying not to sound as desperate as she felt. Just the thought of the world without him in it was more than she could bear.

He stared at her for endless seconds before he cupped her cheeks with his palms. "I promise I'll do my best to see to it that we all come out of this in one piece."

"I'm going to hold you to that." She placed her hands on his lean cheeks, then surprised herself by pressing her lips to his for a quick kiss. When she leaned back, the shocked look on his face made her smile. "I mean business, Mr. Hanson. I don't want anything to happen to you. You keep yourself safe, you hear?"

A slow grin spread across his handsome face. "Yes, ma'am."

Sean stared at the door and windows across the front of the house like a hawk looking for prey, watching for any sign of movement that might be Crowley or one of his cohorts. He was positive that Tom Miller was still in custody, but that didn't mean

Crowley hadn't enlisted more help. They'd never known for sure how many associates he had or how much of a threat any of them were individually. It was anyone's guess who was out there shooting at them. Past experience had taught him to be wary of a decoy attack at the back of the house to disguise the main attack coming at the front. With Crowley anything was within the realm of possibility, and he knew he needed to be ready for any and all situations.

"It's been quiet for a while. Do you think the danger is over?" Bailey asked from his side.

"I would be surprised if it was." He shook his head. "Whoever is out there shot at the back of the house to draw attention away from the front. I'm figuring Crowley or his accomplice will be trying to come through the front door."

"While Thad and Blane are busy returning fire in the kitchen," she said, catching on.

He nodded. "After getting chased off last night, Crowley is going to pull out all the stops this time." When they heard a tap on the door, Bailey jumped and Sean clicked off the safety on his gun.

"Sean, it's me. Sam Fowler," his friend called in a low voice. "Let me in."

"What are you doing here?" he asked, unlocking and opening the door. "How did you know we'd be here and not at Levi's?"

Sam shrugged and joined him and Bailey on the floor behind the couch. "I know what I'd do if I were in your shoes. It makes sense to keep moving around where you have more guns and eyes watching for anything out of the ordinary."

"Miller still in the detention center awaiting arraignment?" Sean asked, wondering why Sam had shown up.

"Yes, and so is his wife," he said, nodding. "Neither one of them is talking, but she made sure her public defender got the court to appoint her mother temporary guardian of the two little boys."

"I'm glad of that," Bailey said, sounding relieved.

Sean stared at Sam as he watched the man's exchange with Bailey. He'd known Sam a long time and he'd never seen him look as tense as he looked at that moment, not even when they'd been pinned down in a shootout. Something wasn't right and when he saw the single trickle of sweat at the man's temple run down to his jaw, every one of his senses went on high alert. Why would Sam be sweating when it was below freezing outside? Unless he was…

"You were in on this all along, weren't you, Sam?" As soon as the words were out, he realized that it made perfect sense. He knew exactly who the mole was in the Cheyenne FBI field office. It had been right under his nose the whole time. Sam's expression was all he needed to see to confirm his suspicion.

"Me? No. You don't know what you're talking about, Hanson." Sweat continued to bead on Sam's forehead and another trickle of sweat joined the first as it ran down the side of his face. "What would make you think I'm in cahoots with Crowley?"

"You're a lousy liar, Sam." Sean shook his head. "You showing up like this without being called and bullets start flying is too much to be coincidence."

"You were the one who put that GPS tracking device on my coat, weren't you?" Bailey scooted closer to Sean as she looked accusingly at the FBI agent whom he'd once called his friend. "I should have guessed that you were the one to do it. When I went to pick up my coat and handbag at the Eagle Fork Sheriff's Department, the sheriff's deputy told me you had put my things in your car at the bank, then later another agent showed up with a story about you 'forgetting' to return them to me."

"You're way too smart for your own good, Ms. O'Keefe." His frustrated expression bore witness to how stretched his nerves were.

"What does Harold Crowley have on you, Agent Fowler?" she demanded. An impressed Sean quickly decided that Bailey would have made a great interrogator. She didn't hesitate to press Sam for answers. "Surely you're not doing this because you *want* Sean to get hurt. I always got the sense that the two of you are close friends."

"Shut up! I don't have a choice." There was anguish in the man's voice, as well as desperation in his eyes. Sam Fowler was trying to keep everything from unraveling and if his desperation was any clue then he was failing miserably.

"What kind of deal did he make with you?" Sean asked, careful to keep his voice calm.

Sam suddenly rose to his feet and pulled his gun. "I told him this wouldn't work. You and your brothers all have enough men on this ranch to guard this entire mountain like it's a fortress."

"Then why did you insist on me taking Ms. O'Keefe up to my cabin?" Sean stood up and held out his hand to Bailey, beckoning her closer to his side as he leveled his own gun on Sam. "You had to know that we wouldn't be vulnerable. My family has owned this mountain too long not to know how to defend it."

"When you talked about it, you didn't mention having a secret way to escape." Sam shook his head. "I figured it would be easy for Crowley and Miller to block off the doors and then..."

"Storm the cabin and kill us," Sean finished for him.

"All Crowley wants is her." Sam pointed his gun at Bailey. "Let me take her with me and you can go back to your cabin and take pictures for the rest of your life for all I care."

"We both know Crowley isn't going to let me live." He motioned for Bailey to get behind him at the same time he saw Blane in his peripheral vision take up position in the hall, his shotgun pointed at Sam's chest. "I've seen his face. You have, too. We both know his MO. We're loose ends that need to be dealt with. Once he kills me, he'll come after you, Sam. You have to know that."

"Shut up! Right now he says all he wants is for me to bring her to him. I don't have a choice any more than..." He stopped and shook his head. "I'm going to take her to him and I can't allow anyone, not even you, Hanson, to stop me." Sam was looking more desperate by the second and Sean realized that he wasn't certain just how far his former friend would take things.

"Then what are you going to do, Sam? Where are you going to go after this is over? There aren't many places to hide when you're a rogue FBI agent on the run." He paused to let his questions sink in. "I can tell you don't want to do this. Why don't we try to figure out a way to resolve it?"

"It's too late." Sam ran a shaky hand over his face as he backed toward the door. "I don't have a choice. Crowley is getting impatient and lives depend on me bringing her to him."

"Lives? Whose lives are you talking about?" So this was a blackmail situation, then. Crowley had to be using someone who meant something to Sam as leverage to get the man to do his dirty work.

"Enough!" Sam roared. "Let me have her now or I swear I'll shoot you and her both."

"No!" Bailey screamed, stepping from behind Sean and just out of his reach. "If you shoot anyone, shoot me. Leave Sean and his brothers alone."

"Bailey, get behind me and let me handle this." His teeth were clenched so tightly his jaw ached. If Fowler pulled the trigger right now, there wasn't a thing he could do to keep her from being shot. She was too far away for him to dive in front of her, and Sam was too far across the room for him to rush forward to grab his gun.

"You've already been shot once because of me. I can't let that happen again." She started forward at the same time Fowler's gun went off and Sean felt his heart drop all the way to his boots.

Bailey screamed, closed her eyes and fell to her knees as she did her best to cover her head with her arms. She didn't think the bullet hit her, but she had so much adrenaline running through her veins, she couldn't tell for sure.

She heard a man yell and what sounded like a door being slammed, then strong hands were scooping her up from the floor. Glancing up, she found herself cradled in Sean's strong arms. "Are you hurt anywhere?" he demanded.

"I don't…think so." She looked around to find herself and Sean were the only ones in the room. "Where did…"

"When his gun went off, I think he thought he had shot you and he took off faster than that mountain lion with his face full of bear spray." Sean lowered her to her feet then pulled her to his chest. "Don't ever do anything like that again." He kissed the top of her head. "I was scared to death that I'd lose you."

Nodding, she took a shaky breath. "Now you know how I felt when you got shot. I didn't want you to get shot again and risk that it would be more than a flesh wound this time." His words that he had been afraid he'd lose her caused her heart to skip a beat, but she reminded herself that they still hadn't talked about the future. She knew he cared about her…but in what way? Did he want a real relationship with her or was he just getting caught up in the drama of their current situation? Could she count on him to be there for her long-term, in a way that no one else had ever been before?

"Where are Blane and Thad?" she asked, to shift the conversation away from her tumultuous feelings.

"They went after Sam, but as fast as he

was moving, I doubt they'll catch him."
He hugged her tight, then released her to
drag the cushions over to put them back on
the couch so they could sit down. "I would
have never thought Sam was the mole in the
Cheyenne office. It just doesn't make sense."

"He kept saying he didn't have a choice,"
she said, trying to figure out why a well-
respected federal agent would be associated
with a notorious criminal. "He said other
lives were at risk, making it seem like if he
didn't go along with helping Crowley something bad would happen."

He nodded. "It's my guess Crowley is
threatening to harm someone Sam cares
about. But there are resources he could have
called on to help him. Allying himself with
a criminal was never his only option—it's
just the option that he chose to take. I've
been trying to think if he's ever given an
indication that he's anything but what he's
represented himself to be and I can't think
of a single time that I've doubted him, not
as an exemplary agent or as a good friend.
Nor did I ever expect him to use our friendship to set me up and then throw me under
the bus."

She gazed down at her hands. "I'm so
sorry."

He looked confused. "Why? You didn't do anything to deserve any of this."

"I'm sorry that you've lost a friend—a man you respected and trusted." She caught her lower lip between her teeth for a moment before she finished. "That has to be unsettling, as well as a huge disappointment. I've only been around him a couple of times, but I thought he was trustworthy, too. I feel betrayed, and I barely even knew him. I can't imagine how it must be for you." She placed her hand on his arm. "Have you been friends for very long?"

He nodded. "I've known Sam since we were both at Quantico for new agent training. I had just received my bachelor's degrees in criminal psychology and communications and Sam had recently been recruited after coming back from serving as a translator in Afghanistan. And you're right. This isn't the Sam I've known for the past twelve years."

"There has to be a reason behind his out-of-character behavior." She frowned. "People normally don't wake up one morning and decide to betray a friendship that's lasted over ten years."

"I have to agree with you. Crowley has to have something on Sam or be threatening him in some way." He stared off into space, then shook his head. "Sam has always been a 'by the book' kind of guy, taking his job very seriously. It would be a pretty big stretch if he gave in to blackmail about his personal conduct. And as far as I know, he doesn't have anyone special in his life that Crowley could use against him. He was married when we were new agents in training, but his wife didn't like the long, sometimes odd, hours that agents have to put in. It put a strain on their marriage and they divorced about a year after we finished our training at Quantico. They didn't have any children and I haven't heard him mention anything about her in years, or anyone else he was interested in, for that matter."

"Could he have met someone recently?" she asked. "After you resigned, how often were the two of you in touch?"

"Every now and then." Sean shrugged. "We stayed friends and stayed in touch."

"And what did you talk about? Which bad guy has moved up on the Most Wanted List?"

He laughed. "We talk about more things than that."

"Oh yeah? What else did you talk about?"

"We both like to fly-fish." He shrugged.

"And Sam sometimes talked about his bowling league."

She rolled her eyes. "No, it certainly doesn't sound like he's out there going to clubs or entertaining a lot. Do you think he might still be close to his ex-wife?"

"Anything's possible." He was thoughtful for a moment. "She does still live down in Denver, about a ninety minute drive away."

Bailey waited for a few minutes before she finally asked, "Are you going to report Agent Fowler to the Denver office?" He'd told her that the Cheyenne office was a satellite office of the main FBI office in Denver.

Sean nodded as he stared off into space. "I have to. I'd be doing the Bureau a huge disservice if I didn't."

Her heart went out to him. Sean didn't want to have to be the one to report his former friend to the authorities, but he was an honorable man and his moral code wouldn't allow him to do anything less. Staring at him for endless seconds, a hint of a smile curved her lips. She really wouldn't want him to be any other way.

TWELVE

At breakfast the next morning, Sean waited until Blane and Thad finished eating and left the house before he made his announcement. "We've had another change of plans, Bailey."

When she eyed him warily over the rim of her coffee cup, he couldn't say he blamed her for her dubious reaction. Over the past week they'd had to switch gears so many times he'd lost count and, although they were pretty certain they had plugged the leaks that had given Crowley so much insight into their movements, they were still no closer to stopping him and Fowler than they were when the nightmare began.

She took a sip from her cup. "Where are we going now?"

"To my place." He got up to rinse his plate and put it in the dishwasher. After refilling his coffee cup, he sat back down beside her at the table. "I have no reason to believe that Sam won't tell Crowley about our moving from house to house on the ranch, which makes it senseless to continue with that plan." He paused and took a deep breath. "I talked to Special Agent in Charge Brad Thompson this morning before you got up. He's the head of the Denver office and I filled him in on what's been going on and who is involved. He agrees that guarding you here on the ranch at my place would be best while he investigates the possibility that other agents in the Cheyenne field office are also involved in the information leak. He was also going to pick up Sam for questioning as soon as possible."

"This is so surreal." She gave him a sad smile. "A week ago we both had friends we were certain we could trust. But here we are."

Nodding, he stared at his coffee. "I'll be the first one to admit, telling Brad Thompson about Sam's association with Crowley was one of the hardest things I've had to do, but I would be just as guilty as he is if I hadn't."

When she gently touched his hand, he looked up and their gazes locked. "Sam, Mary Ann and Tom all made their choices.

Whether they were coerced or willingly went along with Harold Crowley, they all broke the law and they'll all have to pay the price for their bad decisions."

Before he could comment on her observation, his phone rang and the caller ID indicated that it was the Denver FBI office. As soon as he answered, SAC Thompson's voice boomed across the line. "Just wanted to let you know that Special Agent Fowler failed to report for work this morning. One of the marshals sent to pick him up for questioning found a letter of resignation on his office desk."

"So Sam's in the wind." It wasn't a question and Sean didn't expect an answer. "I'm really not surprised. He was pretty upset when he ran out of here last night. I've seen panic before, but Sam took it to a whole new level."

"Yeah, we've been checking things out and it looks like his ex-wife is missing, as well." Brad sighed heavily. "From what we can ascertain, they've been seeing each other off and on for about six months."

"Well, that explains a lot." Sean gave the agent an account of what he knew about the relationship between Sam and his ex. "Last I heard, he hadn't seen her since the divorce and he didn't mention her when he was here six months ago for a fishing trip. But if he's seeing her again and Crowley threatened to harm her, that could very well be the reason he kept telling us that he didn't have a choice."

"I agree." Brad cleared his throat. "I don't know how much good it will do, but I'm going to put out an APB on Fowler."

"If he's thinking straight, he'll probably rent a car and head for Canada." Sean knew of a few quiet little places where it would be easy to slip across the northern border and no one would be the wiser. Sam would know about those, too.

"That sounds about right." He heard someone talking in the background for a few moments before Brad spoke again. "I was just advised that his ex-wife's landlady saw them together this morning. She said they left in a new SUV with out-of-state plates."

"You might want to throw up a few road-blocks along the state line. And tell Home-land Security to alert Border Protection to keep an eye on some of the back roads into Canada." Sean rubbed the tension at the back of his neck. "I remember Sam saying he liked the fishing up in Montana along the northern border so he knows that area pretty well."

"Good to know." When someone else spoke to him, Brad excused himself. "I've got to go, but thanks for the leads. Call me if you think of anything else or if Crowley rears his ugly head again. I'll be in touch if we have news on this end."

"Will do." When he ended the call, Sean reached across the table and took Bailey's hand in his. "I think all of this will be over in a few days."

She nodded. "I didn't mean to listen in on your conversation, but I agree that Crowley must have threatened to harm Agent Fowler's ex-wife."

"It's just private citizen Sam Fowler now. When they went to pick him up for questioning, there was a letter of resignation on his desk." Sean shook his head. "Hard to believe that Crowley is responsible for me and Sam both resigning from the FBI."

The minute the words came out of his mouth, he wanted to take them back. He hadn't intended to tell her the ugly truth about his run-in with Crowley three years ago; hadn't wanted for her to learn about his part in the death of an innocent woman.

* * *

"Both of you?" Bailey felt thoroughly confused. What connection could there be between Sean's resignation and Harold Crowley? "I know why Sam Fowler resigned, but what about you? You resigned because of that awful man, too? What happened?"

He stared down at his boot tops. "If you'll remember I mentioned that Crowley and I have history. I was the negotiator in an earlier robbery where Crowley was holding a hostage captive."

"I think you mentioned it once, but you didn't elaborate on the details." She wondered why negotiating the release of a hostage would cause Sean to give up his career with the FBI. It was something he had trained for and from her experience with his negotiating skills, he was very good at it.

Sean shifted uncomfortably in his seat, and she considered letting the matter drop. She could tell he didn't like talking about it. But on the other hand, she somehow sensed that he needed to, needed to unburden himself of something that weighed him down. "What happened?"

His heavy sigh clued her in to the depth of his ongoing emotional pain tied in with the event. It seemed to her as if something had happened that he hadn't been able to get past. "Crowley took his first hostage in a little town up north called Caney Creek. I was called in to try to get him to release the bank teller and surrender before someone ended up getting hurt."

When he paused, she placed her hand over his where it rested in a tight fist on the top of the table. He'd told her that Earl had been killed because he might have seen Crowley's face. She should have realized that for Sean to know that, he must have seen Crowley react in that way. "He killed the teller because she saw him without his mask, didn't he?" When he flinched, she knew the answer to her question.

"She was married and had two toddlers." He shook his head, and his shoulders slumped as if he carried the weight of the world on them. "I had worked out a deal for him to release her and give himself up, but he'd lied the entire time. He never intended to let her live or to allow us to take him into custody. He shot her and ran out the back door of the bank with the coerced help of a local sheriff's deputy." He grunted. "The man is serving time in a federal penitentiary for being an accessory to murder and bank robbery and won't get out for another five years."

It sent a chill straight up her spine when she realized how similar her situation had been to the poor woman who had lost her life.

"Sean, I know you did everything you could to save that woman's life." She cupped her palms around his fist as she tried to will away the tension gripping him. "Crowley was the one to blame, not you."

"But I was the one who believed he would do what he said, even though I knew better than to trust a criminal." When he raised his gaze to hers, she could see that the guilt he still carried from that day was almost more than he could bear. "I've relived the entire thing over and over, trying to figure out what I could have done differently to save that woman's life, to send her home to her husband and little kids. If I'd been less trusting, less careless. If I'd bothered to put together a backup plan in case Crowley double-crossed us, maybe it all could have worked out. But instead, the day ended in tragedy all because I thought I was a good enough negotiator to talk him into doing the right thing."

She nodded as she continued to stare into

his warm brown eyes. "People like Harold Crowley are ruthless and walk all over the rules. They lie and cheat and, in Crowley's case, kill in an effort to keep themselves from being caught."

He withdrew his hand from hers and stood up to walk over to the sink to look out the window. "You don't understand, Bailey. It was my arrogance and self-assuredness that got her killed. If I hadn't trusted a lowlife like Crowley…"

"Sean Hanson, listen to me," she said, firmly. "You can't blame yourself for what happened. Did you handle the case in Caney Creek by the book?" When he nodded, she gave him a meaningful look. "And you handled the negotiation with Crowley when he held me hostage by the book, as well?"

"Yes, but this time I anticipated that he was lying and that he wouldn't hold up his end of the deal."

"And I'm still alive." She walked over to stand beside him and, putting her hand on his arm, urged him to look at her. "Sean, sometimes God takes the outcome out of our hands. Maybe He decided that it was time for that woman to come home to be with Him."

"You don't understand," he insisted. "Her

kids are growing up motherless because of me."

She stared at him for a moment before she quietly asked, "Did her husband blame you for his wife being killed? Did the FBI blame you for not doing your job?"

"No. Her husband thanked me for doing all that I could to save her," he said, bitterly. "Can you believe that? I failed to get his wife home to him alive and he thanks me." He shook his head. "And the Bureau's review of the case showed no instances of negligence or wrongdoing on anyone's part but the deputy sheriff who helped Crowley."

"So it sounds like no one blames you for the outcome of that negotiation, but you." She rose up on tiptoes to kiss his lean cheek. "If you ask for God's guidance and mercy, you may find that one day you'll be able to forgive yourself, Sean."

Turning, she left the kitchen and went down the hall to the guest bedroom she was using. She wished she could help him get past the terrible events that had taken place the first time his and Harold Crowley's paths had crossed. But only he could do that. And until he stopped blaming himself, there was really nothing more she could do.

* * *

"Thanks for the ride, little brother," Sean said as he got out of the truck and turned to help Bailey. Thad had driven them to the western side of the mountain, continuing the safety measure of their lying down on the backseat of the truck with quilts over them until they pulled into the garage at his place some thirty minutes later.

"If you and your crew will be all right for today, I'll get some sleep and be back over here tonight for guard duty," Thad said, yawning.

"Yeah, most of the activity has been under the cover of darkness." Sean turned to help Bailey from the truck.

"I'll have dinner ready at six," Bailey said, smiling at his youngest brother.

"You can count me in for that." Thad grinned and waved as they started inside the house.

Pushing the button to raise the garage door for his brother to back his truck out, Sean frowned. Bailey had been uncharacteristically silent since their conversation about his part in Crowley's first murder, but she'd been chatty enough with his brothers, apologizing again to Blane about his house being damaged because of her and reminding Thad what time supper would be ready. He missed her usual spontaneous, often amusing commentaries, and wished he could find a way to restore that easy companionship.

What else did you expect, Hanson? He'd told her about his role in a woman's death. Even if she had, in the moment, tried to convince him that it wasn't his fault, after thinking about it, she'd probably decided that he was right, that he *was* to blame for the woman's murder.

"Would you mind me looking through your cabinets to see what I can make for dinner?" she asked, drawing him back to the present as they entered the kitchen.

He pointed to a door on the other side of the room. "The pantry is right over there. If there's something you need and can't find it, let me know and I'll get one of the men to make a grocery run."

"Thank you." She started across the kitchen, then turned back. "Do you mind if I use your washer and dryer? We left most of my clothes behind at your cabin and…"

"Feel free to use whatever you need." When she started to go into the pantry, he added, "If you'll write down sizes and what you'd like in the way of clothing, they can be picked up at the same time as the groceries."

He watched her catch her lower lip between her teeth for a moment before she spoke. "I don't want to impose and I'll gladly pay you back when I can, but there are a few things that would come in handy."

"No problem at all and no, you won't pay me back." He'd give her the moon if he could, but he didn't feel he had the right to tell her that. Not now that she knew why he'd resigned from the FBI. Surely now his attention wouldn't be welcomed. "Just write down what you need and I'll call Sally at the Rancher's General Store. She can include everything you need, from clothes to groceries, and one of the guys will go pick it up."

"If you don't mind, why don't you make the call to put it on your account and then I'll talk to Sally about what I need." Her cheeks colored a pretty pink and he figured that was a pretty good indication that he should let her do the ordering after all.

He nodded. "Just let me know when you have your list ready and we'll make the call."

"Okay. Do you have a preference for dinner tonight?" she asked, opening the door to the pantry.

"The Hanson clan aren't picky eaters."

Thankful that she was talking to him a little more and feeling they were on a more comfortable subject, he laughed. "If we're hungry, we'll eat just about anything you put in front of us."

She grinned. "Hungry enough to gnaw the legs off the table, huh?"

Relieved and happy to hear her joking around, he threw back his head and laughed. "That would be about right."

"Do you and your brothers like Italian food?" she asked from the pantry.

"Who doesn't?"

She walked back into the kitchen. "Do you have a piece of paper and a pen I can use? I'll start the list of food I'll need for the next couple of days. By the way, is Levi coming over for dinner, too?"

"He is if you're going to cook. He was all kinds of upset that he missed supper last night and especially when he found out we didn't save him any cookies." He handed her a notepad and pen from one of the drawers. "By the way, what are we having tonight?"

She looked thoughtful. "How does Caesar salad, garlic bread, giant Italian shells stuffed with an Italian sausage, hamburger and mozzarella cheese mixture, topped with homemade sauce and freshly grated parmesan cheese sound? And for dessert I think I'll make an Italian cream cake and have coffee with Italian sweet cream."

"Wow! That sounds amazing." His mouth began to water at the thought. "I don't think I've ever tried stuffed shells before."

"We lived next door to a wonderful little old Italian lady who passed the recipe on to my mother, then my mother taught me." She smiled. "Most people make them with a ricotta and mozzarella mixture, but Mrs. Pagano preferred to make them with a meat mixture that is so delicious and full of flavor. Once you taste them, you'll never want them any other way."

"Well I'm sold on it already." He loved seeing her smile again.

"Do you mind if I buy for tomorrow evening's dinner, as well?" she asked without looking up from the grocery list she was making.

"Not at all," he answered, pulling out a stool at the kitchen island. "These are the best meals we've had since our mom and dad moved to Arizona."

"Well, I'm glad." She looked up to meet his gaze head-on. "I owe my life to you and your brothers and I want to make sure you all know how much I appreciate everything you've done for me."

When she went back to making her list, he suddenly couldn't imagine his kitchen without her in it, without her cooking a fantastic meal and talking to him while she prepared it. Suddenly feeling like his world had been turned upside down, he decided it was time to put some space between them and find his footing again.

"If you don't mind, I think I'm going to go into my office and call SAC Thompson for an update."

"That will be fine." She raised her head to give him that smile that never failed to send his heart skittering out of control. "I'll let you know when I have my list ready to call in. Oh I'm also going to put you to work this afternoon, being the cook's helper."

He grinned. "Yes, ma'am."

Sean knew he had no right to feel as euphoric as he did. It wasn't going to last. Within a few days Bailey would leave him and the ranch behind to go off on her quest for adventure—a quest she'd probably complete with some guy who'd adore her and appreciate her and never burden her with a dark, troubled past. But she was here with him now and he fully intended to store up as many memories as he could for the days when she was gone and he was alone, longing to have her back.

THIRTEEN

"I think I'm going to pop," Blane said, leaning back in his chair to rub his flat belly. "I thought supper last night was awesome, but I do believe you outdid yourself with this one, Bailey."

Thad groaned. "Well, I could die a happy man right now. I really think you could open a restaurant and it would be a huge success."

"I agree with Thad. You missed your calling, Bailey," Levi added. "You sure know your way around a kitchen."

"I don't even think our mom could match that supper," Sean said, standing to take his and her plates over to the sink. "It really was amazing."

"Thank you. It's a pleasure cooking for such appreciative diners." Bailey smiled. "But don't forget, we have dessert."

Thad stopped groaning and brightened considerably. "Cookies?"

She laughed and shook her head as she pointed to the counter across the room. "We have Italian cream cake and coffee with Italian sweet cream."

"I'm gonna have to join a gym or something," Blane complained good-naturedly.

"Maybe they'll have a family plan and I can hitch a ride with you," Levi said, letting his belt out another notch.

"Tell them what you're going to make for supper tomorrow night," Sean suggested, grinning as he sat back down beside her.

"Tomorrow evening I'm going to make country-fried steaks with milk gravy, mashed potatoes, buttered corn, cowboy beans with bacon and homemade cornbread. And I was thinking about apple pie topped with vanilla bean ice cream and caramel topping for dessert, unless you'd rather have something else."

"Nope. That sounds perfect," Thad said seriously. Turning to Blane, he grinned. "You'd better make plans to come by my place to pick me up when you and Levi go to the gym."

Blane grinned. "I'll drive if you and Levi pay for the gym membership."

"You're cheap, you know that?" Levi's wide grin took the sting out of his jab.

As she listened to the men, she couldn't help but lament the fact that this new nightly tradition of making dinner for them was only temporary. Once Harold Crowley was caught, she'd go back to Eagle Fork and her rented two-bedroom cottage with the white gingerbread trim, on the corner of Pine Street and Chokeberry Lane to eat her meals alone and spend her evenings wishing she was part of a family.

"You're awfully quiet," Sean whispered, leaning close to her ear. "Are you all right?"

She smiled. "I'm just enjoying listening to your brothers' banter. It's really entertaining."

Grinning, he shrugged. "I wouldn't trade them for anything in the world, but I wouldn't give you a nickel for another one just like them, either."

"Spoken like a true older brother," she said, laughing.

"Is anyone ready for coffee and dessert?" she asked, rising to cut the cake.

"I think we should serve you after that delicious supper," Sean said, rising from the chair to take the empty salad bowl from the table. She watched him shoot his brothers a meaningful look that had them all jumping to their feet.

"I'll clear the table," Thad said, taking plates and silverware to the sink to rinse and load into the dishwasher.

"I'm on the coffee," Blane said, reaching into the cabinet for a canister of coffee and a filter.

"Since Levi is the paramedic and into cuts and stuff like that, I think he should cut the cake," Sean said, winking at her as he picked up what was left of the pan of stuffed shells to pack away as leftovers.

"Hey, I repair cuts. I don't make them," Levi complained. His frown suddenly turned into a wicked grin. "But as a matter of fact, I *can* do a decent job when it comes to cutting into a cake."

Thad clapped his hand on Levi's shoulder. "That's because you like to eat cake, bro."

"That's called incentive, little brother," Levi said, cleanly slicing into the white cream cheese icing encrusted with crushed pecans.

Watching the way that they laughed as they worked, she marveled at the four men moving around the kitchen, completely at ease with each other and the domestic chores. Their parents had done a wonderful job of raising them, and she only hoped that she'd one day have children who turned out just like them.

While they all enjoyed dessert, Sean's cell phone rang. Excusing himself from the table he walked into the great room to take the call. Feeling completely at ease with the remaining Hanson brothers, Bailey laughed at a story Levi was telling until she saw Sean's solemn expression when he walked back into the room.

Before she could ask what was wrong, he rubbed the back of his neck, a gesture she'd come to recognize as his way of easing tension. "They just caught Sam Fowler and his ex-wife about fifty miles from the Canadian border. They're going to be detained in Montana until after Crowley is caught."

"Was his ex in on all this, too?" Blane asked, taking a bite of cake.

Sean shook his head. "She's being put in protective custody." He nodded at Bailey. "It was just as we suspected. Crowley had threatened Sam's ex-wife in order to get his cooperation. He was trying to protect her."

"But why didn't he just report what was happening and let the authorities put Crowley under arrest?" To her that made more sense than losing his position with the FBI, throwing away his friendship with Sean and jeopardizing her and Sean's lives.

"Men in love don't always think straight, nor do they make solid decisions," Levi offered, his voice strangely subdued. For the first time since she'd met them, none of the brothers teased Levi about his comment and it was clear there was a reason why. The man had obviously been in a relationship that hadn't ended well.

"Well, I hope they go easy on him," Bailey said, pensively. "He was doing all the wrong things but he was acting out of what I'm sure he thought were the right reasons."

"Thompson said Sam's cooperating and that will go in his favor." Sean placed his hand over hers resting on the table and his warm touch made her feel more secure. "With Sam's help, I'm sure Crowley will be caught within another day or two."

Bailey watched as the men resumed their previous conversation and the banter that she'd come to associate with the brothers. She withdrew just a bit, thinking about what this meant—the prospect of Crowley getting caught in just another day or two.

She would be glad not to be afraid anymore, not to worry about walking outside in the daylight for fear of being gunned down.

She would be free to go on with her life and her resolve to experience new and exciting things. But her freedom would come with a price and that was losing contact with Sean.

Suddenly needing to be alone before she did something dumb like break down and cry, she forced a smile, pulled her hand from beneath Sean's and stood up. "I'm a little tired and if you all don't mind, I think I'm going to turn in for the night."

The brothers all stood up and bid her good-night as she left the kitchen, except for Sean. He followed her across the great room and down the hall to her guest room.

"Are you sure you're all right?" he asked when they stopped at the door.

"It's been a pretty eventful week and I haven't been sleeping very well." She shrugged one shoulder. "As far as I can tell, you haven't been sleeping much at all."

"I'll be all right." His dismissal of his own needs was both touching and infuriating. On one hand, his selflessness was one of the things she adored about him. On the other, she wanted him to take better care of his own well-being, to stop dwelling on the past and start to live again.

She placed her palm on his square jaw and as she stared into his warm brown eyes, she knew that her life would be hollow without him. "Sleep well, Sean."

Pulling his head down as she rose up on her tiptoes, she brushed her lips across his, then went inside the bedroom and closed the door behind her. She didn't want him to see her cry; didn't want him to know that at some point along the journey, she'd lost her heart and fallen completely and hopelessly in love with him.

Sean felt like he was waiting for the other shoe to drop. Crowley was sure to make a move now that he no longer had Tom Miller and Sam Fowler doing his dirty work. And Agent Thompson had advised him that Fowler had assured them Crowley didn't have any more henchmen for them to worry about. Now the only question was where and when he'd try something on his own. He had to be feeling that time was running out before the FBI caught up with him.

Walking down the hall, carrying his boots to keep from disturbing Bailey, he crossed the great room to enter the kitchen and found his brothers playing a game of rummy. "It's five in the morning and you're playing cards?" Grinning, he shook his head. "Must have been a pretty peaceful night. At least you have a pot of coffee made."

"Yeah, we've got more caffeine in our veins than blood cells at this point," Blane said, laying down four aces. "Rummy, boys!"

"Well, that's it for me." Thad picked up the cards to put back in the cardboard pack. "I'm going to make another sweep of the barn and stable and ask the men if they've seen anything, then I'm heading back to my place. I'm on duty tonight for emergency calls at the veterinary clinic in Cheyenne, so I won't be able to come over until I get off at seven tomorrow morning."

"Watch out for those wild ones, Dr. Dolittle," Levi said, standing up to stretch as Thad left. "It was a pretty quiet night, nothing going on. We were speculating that Crowley may have cut his losses and headed for the border like Sam Fowler did."

Sean shook his head. "I don't think so. He's the type who doesn't quit unless it's on his terms."

"In other words, he's not going to give up until he's caught or you and Bailey are dead," Blane said, his expression grim.

"That's about the size of it." Sean sat down to pull on his boots. "He has to be getting desperate now that his accomplices are sitting it out behind bars."

"Are you expecting him to make a move soon?" Levi asked, draining his coffee cup to set it in the sink.

"I expect it within the next day or so," Sean admitted as he poured some coffee for himself. "Crowley's an opportunist and if he thinks he has the advantage, he's not likely to plan out his next move. He'll just act. I think he's watching this place and waiting for the moment he thinks our guard is down."

"You think he'll try something when Levi and I leave this morning?" Blane asked, all traces of humor gone.

"It's possible." He shrugged. "But I intend to take some more precautions just in case."

"What do you want us to do?" Levi asked. "Say the word and it's as good as done."

"Why don't you bunk down here today? I'm going to get in touch with Brad Thompson and find out how he wants to proceed with his investigation. He may have made a decision about whether he wants us to stay put or move to one of the safe houses in Cheyenne."

"What would his reasoning be for that?" Blane asked.

"He's said before that moving Bailey to a

safe house would draw Crowley away from the ranch and stop him from causing damage the Bureau has to pay for." He shook his head. "But I'm against that plan. I don't like the idea of using her to bait Crowley. Just because Sam says none of the other agents are involved, doesn't mean Crowley hasn't solicited someone else to help. And with that potential problem, on top of the other issues that come part and parcel with safe houses, there are too many things that could go wrong. She could get hurt or worse."

"Do I have a say in the matter?" Bailey asked, walking into the room.

He hadn't meant for her to overhear the conversation, but now that she had, she could tell Thompson herself that it was out of the question. "Of course you do," Sean said, rising to hold her chair.

Once she was seated, Blane poured her a cup of coffee and set it on the table in front of her. "We want this over with, don't we?" she asked, looking from one Hanson brother to another. When they all nodded uneasily, she took a sip of her coffee. "Then I say let's do it. I'll go to a safe house and be the bait if that's what it takes to end this so that you can all go back to your lives here on the ranch."

Sean couldn't believe she was willing to go along with Thompson's scheme. "Bailey, you don't understand…"

"I understand perfectly well." She gently placed her hand on his arm where the bullet wound was healing. "I don't want any of you to get shot—much less shot again. I don't want you to have your houses destroyed, or barns set on fire, or your vehicles sabotaged or anything else this awful man comes up with to try to get to me."

"Bailey, I can't let you do this." As far as he was concerned, any plan that used her as bait was off the table. "You could be hurt or worse and I couldn't bear it if that happened."

He saw Levi tap Blane on the shoulder, then they both got up and quietly left the house. He appreciated their consideration, letting him and Bailey have this conversation with some privacy, but wasn't surprised by it. They could prank, tease and give each other a hard time, but they knew when to back off, as well.

"You'll have to be with me at the safe house, won't you? You're one of his targets, too."

"Yes, but there are still too many ways that things could go sideways."

She took his hand in her much smaller one. "I know you want this over so you can get back to taking pictures at that beautiful cabin of yours on top of the mountain. If this plan works out, that will happen."

"Something could go wrong and I'm not willing to take that chance," he insisted. He had to make her see that the chance for success was all but nonexistent and definitely not worth the risk. "Your safety and well-being are more important to me than taking pictures. The animals will still be there next week or next month or however long it takes to do this right."

"Why, Sean? Why is my well-being so important to you?" Her intense gaze made him look away.

"Because…it's my job to see that you're safe." As soon as he said it, he wanted to take it back. The hurt look on her face made him feel like he'd been punched in the gut. She was much more to him than just a job, even if he didn't have the right to lay the claim on her that he wanted. "Bailey, I didn't mean that the way it sounded."

She withdrew her hand and nodding, stood up. "I, um, I'm not really hungry this morning." Turning to go back down the hall, she added, "Don't forget to tell Special Agent Thompson that I'll be the bait he needs to catch Harold Crowley."

When she disappeared into her room, he wanted to kick himself for being such a bonehead. He hadn't meant for the take-away from his statement to be that she was just a job to him. That was the furthest thing from the truth. The truth was that he loved her, even if he knew he couldn't ask for her love in return.

His heart came to a full stop, then took off beating so fast that he had to catch his breath. He loved her? As the thought swept through him with a warmth that settled in his chest, he knew as surely as he knew his own name that it was true. He loved Bailey; she had become his world. But no matter what anyone said, he knew she deserved a whole lot better than the likes of him.

Please, God, if I can't talk her out of this and something goes wrong, please take me instead of her.

FOURTEEN

"Well, this isn't too bad," Bailey said to herself as she looked around the small safe house that Special Agent Thompson had taken her and Sean to. Whoever had decorated the place had certainly been a minimalist, but there was enough room on the shabby, uncomfortable-looking couch for her and Sean to sit, and the table in the kitchen had two chairs. As far as kitchen storage went there was just enough room in the two white enameled cabinets above the sink for the four-serving set of chipped dishes and mismatched cups. The sink, she was certain, had to be from the 1930s, and was supported by two ugly, tarnished chrome legs with an apartment-size refrigerator on one side and a microwave on a rolling cart on the other.

On further inspection of the interior, she found there were two bedrooms of equal size with just enough room for a twin-size bed, and a bathroom that looked like it had once been a small closet. Every room needed a new coat of paint and the carpets all had spots where the warp was showing through. All in all, most people's first apartment looked better, but it seemed to be clean enough and since they would only be there a night or two, it shouldn't be too bad.

As she strolled back into the living room, she overheard what seemed to be a heated conversation between Sean and Special Agent Thompson taking place outside on the front porch. She wasn't certain, but she had a good idea they were arguing over her decision to be the bait. She sighed, wishing Sean would let this fight go. It wasn't that she was all that brave and unconcerned about what might happen. In truth, she was terrified. But even greater than her fear was her need to resolve this mess so they could start putting Crowley behind them.

Sean needed to forget all about the horrible man and the murder he had committed three years ago. It still haunted him, and she got the sense that nothing would resolve that until he could get some closure by catching Crowley and seeing him brought to justice. If that was true, then she was willing to risk her life to bring him what little bit of peace she could.

Lost in thought she jumped when the door suddenly opened and Sean walked into the tiny living room. "Agent Thompson and I agreed to a deadline. If this isn't resolved within two days, we will be going back to the ranch to await Crowley's next move."

She nodded. "How is this going to work? Will someone tell Crowley that we've been moved to a safe house here in Cheyenne?"

"He probably already knows," Sean admitted. "I'm sure he was watching when Thompson and the marshals showed up with the transfer van." When their gazes met, the warmth in his brown eyes took her breath away. "He probably followed us here."

"Do we have guards outside?" Surely, if they were going to catch the criminal, they'd need someone outside to actually make the arrest before Crowley had the chance to get into the house.

"That's another thing I'm not overly happy about. There is one agent at the back of the house, two at the front in an unmarked car and surveillance cameras on both sides of the house, sending a live feed to a van down the street where the rest of the team is on standby. And if he gets past everyone else, I'm the last line of defense."

"I'm sure they'll catch him outside," she said, trying to convince herself as much as she tried to convince him.

"Let's hope so." He walked over to part the drapes and look out at the car with the two agents parked along the curb. "It's going to be dark soon and unless he changes his MO, we should be getting a visit from him sometime between sundown and midnight."

She nodded. "Unless he failed to see us leave the ranch."

"Yup." He put the drapes back in place and walked the twenty feet to the back door. "But I'm sure he knows exactly where we are. He's too persistent to have let his surveillance drop. I'd imagine he also knows that agents are positioned around the house, ready for a showdown."

Sensing that talking about this was only getting him more worked up, she decided to change the subject. "I hope your brothers weren't too disappointed about dinner tonight," she said, glancing at the grease-spotted bags of fast food sitting on the kitchen table that Agent Thompson had brought them for dinner.

"They'll survive." Sean paced from the back to the front of the house and she realized that he wouldn't be distracted from his anxieties that easily.

"He's not so worried now about me seeing his face during the robbery, is he? So many people were there that day. He has to know they all could identify him. This has turned into a vendetta for him." When Sean nodded, a shiver slithered up her spine.

"He's not worried about you testifying in court," he explained. "Crowley has decided in his twisted mind that you and I are to blame for him getting arrested in the first place—and therefore, we must be punished."

"In other words, we made him angry so now we have to pay?" What kind of warped logic was that?

"Something like that." He sounded completely distracted as he rubbed the back of his neck. "Listen, we should have a plan for what to do if it comes down to Crowley getting ahold of you and me having to point my gun at him. If I give you a nod, I want you to immediately go completely limp and drop to the floor."

"Okay. What happens after that?" she asked, afraid she already knew.

His expression was completely emotionless when he answered her question. "I'll take the shot that will end this thing for good."

Lying on the instrument of torture the FBI called a mattress, Sean stared at the ceiling and wondered what Crowley was up to and where he was. Wherever that might be, Sean was sure it wasn't too far away.

When he turned to his side, he listened for any movement, but everything was quiet, with the exception of an occasional vehicle passing by outside. Bailey had turned in shortly after he'd told her he wouldn't hesitate to take the shot that would end Crowley's life. It wasn't something he wanted to do—he was grateful that he hadn't had to do it in all of his years with the Bureau—but that didn't mean he couldn't or wouldn't do it. Harold Crowley was violent and dangerous and needed to be stopped, but Sean had no illusions that the man would be taken into custody easily. If he put up a fight, killing him might be the only possible way to stop him from harming someone else.

When he heard the sound of someone moving around in Bailey's room, he realized that he must have drifted off. Instantly awake, he reached for his gun on the nightstand beside the bed, sat up and listened intently for any indication it wasn't Bailey just being restless. He breathed a sigh of relief when he heard the bathroom door open. Once she went back to bed, he'd get up to do a check of the house and make sure everything was still secure, with the agents outside still in position.

When he heard the other bedroom's door close, he released the safety on his gun and got up. As quietly as he could, he walked into the living room to look out the front window. It appeared nothing was happening that was out of the ordinary. Both agents were in the front seat of the car and appeared to be drinking coffee and eating something. Probably donuts—always a popular choice for a stakeout. He couldn't help but smile. He'd spent his rookie year with the FBI drinking coffee and eating stale donuts. As he walked the short distance to the back door, the hairs on the back of his neck stood up and a sinking feeling settled in his gut. The door was slightly open, with about an inch of space between the edge of the door and the doorjamb. Someone had either entered or left the house and failed to pull the door shut.

He knew for certain that Bailey wouldn't have gone outside. Turning toward the bedrooms, he stopped short at the sight of Bailey facing him with Harold Crowley's arm around her neck in a choke hold. The sorry excuse for a human being had her pulled to his chest, using her as a shield the way he'd done on the day of the robbery. The only difference between that day and now was the silencer attached to the barrel of the gun he held. Apparently, he'd finally gotten one.

"Hello, Hanson," Crowley growled, his sinister grin revealing a mouthful of tobacco-stained teeth as he forced Sean to take several steps backward into the living room. "Looks like the cat finally caught the mice."

"How did you get in here?" Sean demanded, making sure the Glock 9 millimeter pistol in his hand was pointed directly between the man's eyes. He needed to keep Crowley talking while he assessed the situation and came up with a plan that put Bailey in the least amount of danger.

"Let's just say the agent facedown in the backyard won't be working for the FBI anymore." His laughter was maniacal and the wild look in his eyes hinted that he was hyped up on some kind of drug. "A stun gun and a lethal dose of ketamine guarantees he's on a permanent leave of absence."

Bailey gasped in horror at the callous way Crowley talked about killing the agent, causing him to tighten his arm across her throat. Sean watched helplessly as she choked and struggled for her next breath. "That's enough, Crowley!" he barked out. "You know you're not going to get away with this."

"Watch me. But you're right about one thing, *former* Special Agent Hanson. It's time to wrap this up. I've wasted enough time on you two." Crowley mocked him, but Sean noticed with some relief he did ease the pressure on Bailey's neck. "I want her to watch you die first so she knows there's no more chances, no more heroic moves coming out of nowhere to save her."

"Mr. Crowley…before you carry out… this senseless act of violence… I have one question. Why did you…kill Earl McKenzie?" Bailey asked, struggling to breathe. "He didn't see…your face."

"He tore off my mask and made me have to kill you and Hanson," the man said as if his logic made perfect sense. "All this could have been avoided if he'd left well enough alone and let me take the money and get away. But no, he had to play the hero for you." He sneered as he looked at Bailey, making Sean want to rearrange his face. "What is there about you that makes men want to be heroes?" He shrugged dismissively. "I don't get it. You're just as worthless as every other woman…"

"Stop right there," Sean said, glaring at the man who had just insulted the woman he loved more than his own life. Harold Crowley could make fun of him all he wanted to, call him whatever he liked, but the lowlife had better not make another disparaging remark about Bailey.

"Oh so that's the way the wind blows." Crowley leaned his head closer to Bailey's. "You got yourself a boyfriend out of all this, didn't you, little sister? Too bad neither one of you is going to live long enough to see where this romance goes."

Sean could hear the impatience in Crowley's raspy voice and knew time was running out. The man couldn't afford to spend much more time talking if he wanted to make a clean getaway after he killed them.

"Bailey, do you remember what I told you earlier this evening?" Sean asked, giving her a meaningful smile he hoped Crowley would think was a reference to a romantic secret shared between the two of them. He knew the moment she understood by the determined look in her expressive green eyes. "Me, too," he said, nodding.

Crowley was apparently distracted by the exchange between them and when she went as limp as a wet rag, just as they'd planned, the unexpected extra weight on his forearm was more than Crowley could support. She fell to the floor in a heap at the man's feet before he could manage to catch her. Crowley roared with rage and started to point his gun at her. That was when Sean took the shot that he hoped would put an end to Crowley's reign of terror and land him in jail for the rest of his miserable life.

Bailey felt as if her heart stopped when Harold Crowley landed with a hard thump on the floor next to her, his groans of pain echoing in her ears. As she scrambled to her feet, Sean rushed forward to kick Crowley's gun out of his reach and to keep his own sidearm aimed at the man to prevent Crowley from reaching for his weapon or anything else he could use to do harm. Without thinking twice she rushed into his arms and held on for dear life.

"It's over, Bailey. You're finally safe."

One strong arm closed around her and held her close while he kept the gun trained on Crowley. Burying his face in her silky hair, he took a deep breath. "Are you all right?" He leaned back to look at her, shifting his gaze constantly between her and Crowley. "Are you breathing okay? We should probably have you checked out by a doctor."

"I'm fine, thanks to you." Wrapping her arms around his waist, she rested her head on his chest. "I was so afraid you were going to have to kill him."

The deep breath he released ruffled her hair. "I thought it would come to that, too. But I managed to redirect my aim at the last second and disable him by shooting him in the shoulder instead. I don't want his death on my conscience, but I do believe he needs to spend the rest of his life in a prison cell with plenty of time to reflect on what he's done."

She jumped when the front and back doors both burst open at the same time and the house was flooded with FBI agents and US Marshals with guns drawn. One of them immediately put shackles on Harold Crowley's ankles to keep him from getting up and trying to run, while another picked up the gun he'd used and after reengaging the safety, put it into a plastic zippered bag and labeled it as evidence. Special Agent Thompson walked in shortly after the other agents came charging in, looking quite pleased with himself.

"Well, it looks like we got him," he said, smiling.

Bailey was incensed that the agent was taking credit when Sean was the one who had actually dealt with Crowley. "Excuse me? What exactly did you do besides put us in this house as bait? Shouldn't you be congratulating Mr. Hanson? He's the one who kept me safe and apprehended Harold Crowley for you."

The man looked as surprised as if she'd slapped him. "Well, I...um, of course Sean was instrumental in taking Crowley down..."

"No. Don't downplay it like that. He wasn't just helpful in your efforts to catch this awful man. He did it for you, by himself, without an agent in the room." She folded her arms across her chest. "I believe in giving credit where it's due. Sean deserves the recognition for a job well-done." She raised one eyebrow as she gazed up at the agent. "Don't you agree, Special Agent in Charge Thompson?"

Holding up his hands as if to fend off another lecture, he nodded. "You're right. I give you my word. Hanson will get all of the public credit for taking down Crowley. The Bureau owes you our thanks, Hanson. Job well-done."

When he turned to speak to one of the US Marshals handcuffing Harold Crowley to an ambulance gurney, Sean placed his hands on her shoulders and stared at her. "You really didn't have to do that. I don't need accolades or recognition for doing my job."

Her heart felt as if it shattered into a million pieces. Even after what he'd said before, she'd still held on to some hope that she was more to him than just a job. But now he had, once again, put into words what she'd known all along. She was, and always would be, nothing more than an assignment, someone to protect and save from the bad guys.

Someone to leave behind for good now that the assignment was over.

"With Crowley in custody, will I be able to go home now?" she asked, her eyes focused on the ratty carpeting on the floor, refusing to allow him to see the tears threatening to spill down her cheeks.

Frowning, he nodded. "I'll ask, but I thought you might want to come back to the ranch for tonight. I could drive you in to Eagle Fork in the morning."

"I think it would be for the best if I just go on home." She forced a smile that probably looked more like a grimace. Under the circumstances, it was the best she could manage. "I've imposed on you and your brothers long enough."

"Bailey, you haven't been…"

She shook her head and cut him off. "I need to get back to see about Earl's wife, Mavis, as well as figure out what I want to do next."

He continued to stare at her for several long moments before he gave a single nod. "If that's what you really want, I'll tell Thompson."

It wasn't what she wanted, but it was what she needed in order to survive.

FIFTEEN

Three days after Sean had said goodbye to Bailey and watched the US Marshals drive her away to her house in Eagle Fork, he found himself wandering through his home feeling like a stranger, out of sorts and completely lost. Nothing looked right or felt like it should and he knew exactly what the problem was. Bailey wasn't with him. Considering she had only spent a little over twenty-four hours in the house, it didn't make sense that her absence would leave such a void, but that didn't change the fact that it just wasn't the same place without her. He hadn't even been able to drink his morning coffee or eat a meal at the table without thinking about her moving around his kitchen like she owned it. *Just like she owns your heart.*

Glancing at the small bag of her things she'd had to leave behind when they fled the cabin reminded him that his mountaintop retreat didn't feel any better or more comfortable to him than the house. He'd made the hike up there yesterday to retrieve her belongings and make sure the cabin was secure. It had felt so lonely, he'd straightened up, locked it down and hiked right back down to his truck parked at the trailhead to come home. He closed his eyes against his inner pain at the thought that he'd never again get to hold her, never get to spend another day listening to her and being amused and fascinated by the world according to Bailey O'Keefe.

He rubbed a hand at the tension collecting at the base of his neck as he sat down at his desk. Everything had been going pretty well until he'd told her about the first time Harold Crowley had killed and the part he'd played in it. Thinking back on it now, he realized that some of the guilt he'd carried with him for the past three years had finally lifted. Knowing that Crowley wouldn't be able to hurt anyone else made it a little easier for him to let go of his self-recriminations.

Would Bailey be able to forgive him for that old failure? Now that his guilt wasn't so overwhelming, he started to wonder if he'd misread her reaction. She'd withdrawn after he'd told her, and he'd assumed it was because she'd blamed him, even though she'd claimed to believe it wasn't his fault. But had it really been her withdrawal...or his? Had he spent so much time punishing himself that he'd seen a rejection she'd never intended?

He remembered her words. She'd told him he wasn't to blame, that the career criminal was solely responsible for the woman's death. Was she right? He had conducted the negotiation by the book and it still had a bad outcome. Could it be that it was as Bailey said, that it had been the woman's time, that the reason she died was because the Lord had called her home to be with Him, not because of anything he had or hadn't done?

God, if Bailey is right, that it was Your will for that woman to die, please show me Your mercy and lift the rest of this burden I've carried the past three years.

As he sat there staring off into space a peaceful, easy feeling slowly began to settle within his soul, replacing the lingering guilt with a sense of love and forgiveness. He wasn't sure how long he sat there marveling at God's grace and thanking Him for helping Sean break free of his inner struggle, when he heard the back door open and boots begin to tromp through the kitchen.

"Sean?" Levi called.

"In my office." Rising to his feet, he met his brothers in the great room. "What's up?"

Thad glared at him. "We've come to tell you what a bonehead you are."

"Yeah, Methuselah. If you're too old for that girl, I'll eat your hat in the middle of Main Street in Eagle Fork and give your thirty minutes to gather a crowd to watch," Blane added, sounding disgusted.

Levi shrugged. "What they said, times two."

"When Bailey was here you were more yourself than we'd seen in years." Blane grinned. "It reminded us of the brother you used to be before you became a picture-taking hermit, hiding up on the top of Cougar Mountain."

Thad nodded. "And besides, Bailey's a good cook."

"Down, little brother," Levi said, slapping Thad's shoulder in a good-natured gesture. "But seriously, Sean, that girl is good for you. She makes you happier than we've seen you in a month of Sundays."

"Would it bother any of you if I had a say in the matter?" Sean asked, unable to stop grinning. He felt more free than he had in years.

"Well, sure, but…" Blane stopped to give him a suspicious look. "What's wrong with you? You're grinning like a bear with his paw in a jar full of honey."

Sean looked down at his boots, took a deep breath and nodded. "I had to figure some things out and ask for some guidance from the Man upstairs. I like where He led me—and I think I know where I'm going now."

"We're glad to hear it," Levi said, being the first to give him a brotherly hug.

"I'm just glad to get my big brother back," Blane said, taking his turn to hug Sean.

Thad stepped up and, grinning, pulled Sean into a bear hug. "So what are you waiting for? Go get her, bro."

Feeling younger than he had in years, Sean didn't waste time grabbing the bag of things Bailey had left at the cabin, shrugging into his coat and digging his truck keys out of his jeans pocket. He had one shot to get this right and he wasn't about to blow it.

Bailey left Mavis McKenzie's house after taking Earl's widow a plate of spaghetti with meatballs and marinara sauce, garlic bread and a tossed salad. Mavis was devastated over Earl's passing, and Bailey was trying every way she could to help the woman cope with her overwhelming loss.

As she walked the three blocks to her rented house on Chokeberry Lane, she couldn't help but notice how much colder it was in Wyoming than it was back home in southern Illinois. There was already several inches of snow covering the ground and she'd been told that a white Christmas was all but guaranteed every year. As she crossed the street and walked toward her little house, she looked at all of the houses decorated with colorful Christmas lights and couldn't help wondering if Sean and his brothers would travel to celebrate the holiday with their parents in Arizona. Or would they stay home and get together? She sighed and brushed a tear from her cheek. Who would cook Christmas dinner for them?

Gazing up at the night sky, she wondered where he was and what he was doing. Was he looking up at the same stars and wondering about her? Probably not. He'd probably put her out of his mind and started planning his next trip up to his cabin to take pictures of the wild animals.

She sighed as she opened the front fence

gate and started up to the porch. Tonight she would decide where to move to next and start checking things off the bucket list she'd made after she'd returned home from the safe house in Cheyenne. The wonderful little town of Eagle Fork had been a great place to start the next chapter in her life and it had started to feel like a place that she might want to make her home for the rest of her life, but that was no longer a possibility. As small as it was, she would eventually cross paths with Sean or his brothers and it would be a painful reminder of the life she wanted but would never have.

Just as she climbed the steps and walked across the porch to her front door, a big crew-cab truck pulled up to the curb in front of the house. Her heart skipped a beat as she watched Sean get out and walk up to the house with that loose-limbed cowboy gait that made her stomach flutter. She'd never seen him look more handsome and that spelled big trouble for her already broken heart.

"Good evening, Bailey," he said, his smile stealing her breath away. When he climbed the steps, she couldn't seem to find her voice. "Do you mind if I come in for a few minutes?" he asked when she continued to silently stare at him.

"Oh uh…of course," she said, pulling out her keys. She tried to open the door herself, but her hands were shaking. Sean stepped in to unlock the door for her. She preceded him into the house and couldn't help but wonder what on earth he was doing there. "Would you like some coffee?"

"No, thanks." He handed her a bag. "I went up to the cabin and got all of the things you had to leave behind."

"Oh right. Thank you," she said, setting it on the couch.

"I also have a little news I think you'll want to hear," he said, smiling. "Tom and Mary Ann Miller are cooperating with the investigation—and we finally found out how they're connected to Crowley. It turns out, Harold Crowley is Tom's older stepbrother and threatened to harm their little boys if they didn't go along with his scheme to rob the bank."

"Oh that's terrible." She shook her head. "I know it was wrong, but I really can't blame them for trying to protect their babies. I'm not sure I wouldn't have done the same thing."

She watched him look around at her modest little house with stacks of boxes she'd collected that afternoon to pack her things in. "Are you going somewhere?"

She nodded. "I'm getting ready to move."

His gaze was intense when he captured hers. "Why?"

"After what happened at the bank, I decided that I'd rather use my accounting degree doing taxes or helping people manage their finances."

"That doesn't sound very adventurous or exciting," he said, his low voice causing her insides to quiver.

"Actually, I've decided that adventurous and exciting are overrated and might not be for me," she said, shrugging one shoulder.

When he stepped in front of her and put his large hands on her shoulders, she barely managed to keep her tears from betraying the state of her emotions. "I thought you might like to experience a few new and exciting adventures with me around the ranch."

She stared at the open snap on the collar of his chambray shirt. "Sean… I don't think…that's a good idea."

"Why, Bailey?"

"After the past week and a half, you have to ask?"

Stepping closer, until he was just inches

away from her, he said, "I can understand why you might think I'd be the wrong person for a fun adventure, given how weighed down by guilt I've been this whole time. But you were right. God and I had a long talk about my involvement in that negotiation with Crowley three years ago. He had mercy on me and with His help I finally accepted that some things are out of my hands and that He's in control."

"I think that's wonderful that you've come to terms with it and it's always the best thing to ask for God's guidance and help, but why are you telling me, Sean? You said yourself that I was just a job, and that job's over now."

He kissed her forehead then shook his head. "No, sweetheart. I said it was my job to protect you—and that job will *never* be done." He used his index finger to tip her chin up until they were staring into each other's eyes. "That's what a man does—protect the woman he loves."

Her heart came to a full stop, then raced as if she was running for a finish line. "You love me?"

His smile was all it took to cause her tears to flow freely down her cheeks. "Yes, ma'am." He wiped away a tear with the pad of his thumb. "I think I fell in love with you the first moment I heard your voice on the phone the day of the bank robbery."

She sniffled and accepted the handkerchief he pulled from his jeans pocket. "I love you, too, Sean. More than you'll probably ever know."

"Then I have something to ask you," he said, giving her a smile that stole her breath. "Will you go with me to the Christmas Jubilee next Saturday night?"

Happiness swept over her and she snuggled against his wide chest. "Are you asking me out on a date, Mr. Hanson?"

His deep laughter caused a warmth to radiate throughout her being. "Yes, ma'am."

When he settled his lips over hers in a heartfelt kiss that made her head spin, she felt as if she'd finally found her place in the world at the side of the man she'd waited for her entire life.

EPILOGUE

In early summer Bailey found herself galloping across the valley toward the line shack on the beautiful chestnut mare Sean had given her for her birthday in the spring. With the wind in her hair and Sean riding his big bay gelding beside her, she thanked God for the many blessings she'd received since moving to Wyoming.

She laughed when she thought of the bucket list she'd made the day after she'd gotten home from the safe house in Cheyenne, the list she'd committed to memory the day Harold Crowley had held her hostage. She'd lost that list, but it didn't matter. She had done almost all of the things on it and had experienced more excitement and adventure in the past several months than she had in her entire life. Just a week ago she'd camped out with Sean and his parents—in town for a visit—in this same valley and they'd gazed up at the wide Wyoming sky with its endless stars that seemed almost close enough to touch. And now she had ridden her very own horse across the mountain meadow, the very meadow they'd hiked across to escape a ruthless madman.

When they stopped beside the river winding across the upland valley, Sean dismounted and reached up to lift her down from the mare. He gave her a kiss that curled her toes inside her new Western boots, then tilted his head to stare down at her. "Have I told you lately how pretty you look and how much I love you?"

"Only about ten times today, but I never get tired of hearing it," she said, smiling as she wrapped her arms around his waist. "I love you, too, cowboy."

He kissed her forehead before stepping back to pull a blanket and the thermal pack with their lunch from his saddlebags. Together they walked over to a spot beneath a large birch tree. When he set the blanket and pack down, she wondered what he was up to. He normally couldn't wait to find out what she'd packed for their picnic, but he didn't seem all that interested today.

After pulling a piece of paper from his shirt pocket, he handed it to her. It was the list she'd made when she got home from the safe house; the list she'd thought she lost. "Well, it looks like we've checked off all but a couple of things on your list," he said. "I made sure you got to camp out under the stars so you could see the night sky and today you got to ride your horse across the valley and feel the wind in your hair. We love each other, and although I can try until the end of time, I'll never be good enough for you." He smiled as he took her hands in his and dropped to one knee. "Would you do me the honor of marrying me and maybe a year or so from now start on that beautiful family you want?"

Tears of joy filled her eyes and she suddenly found herself completely speechless when he pulled a black velvet box from his pocket and opened it. Inside was a white gold engagement ring with a gorgeous solitaire diamond. She'd hoped for this day, with this man, but she'd never dreamed he would make it so romantic or that he'd make sure she got to do everything on her bucket list.

When she continued to marvel at what a wonderful and caring man he was, he cleared his throat. "Bailey, sweetheart, don't leave me hanging here," he said, grinning. "Will you marry me?"

Grinning, she knelt down on her knees to face him and placed her hands on the cheeks of the man she loved with all her heart. "Yes, sir. I can't wait to be your wife."

* * * * *

HARLEQUIN SELECTS COLLECTION

19 FREE BOOKS IN ALL!

RaeAnne Thayne — A COLD CREEK HOMECOMING

LINDA LAEL MILLER — SIERRA'S HOMECOMING

MOUNTAIN SHERIFF

From Robyn Carr to RaeAnne Thayne to Linda Lael Miller and Sherryl Woods we promise (actually, GUARANTEE!) each author in the Harlequin Selects collection has seen their name on the *New York Times* or *USA TODAY* bestseller lists!

YES! Please send me the **Harlequin Selects Collection**. This collection begins with 3 FREE books and 2 FREE gifts in the first shipment. Along with my 3 free books, I'll also get 4 more books from the Harlequin Selects Collection, which I may either return or keep for the low price of $24.14 U.S./$28.82 CAN. each plus $2.99 U.S./$7.49 CAN. for shipping and handling per shipment*.If I decide to continue, I will get 6 or 7 more books (about once a month for 7 months) but will only need to pay for 4. That means 2 or 3 books in every shipment will be FREE! If I decide to keep the entire collection, I'll have paid for only 32 books because 19 were FREE! I understand that accepting the 3 free books and gifts places me under no obligation to buy anything. I can always return a shipment and cancel at any time. My free books and gifts are mine to keep no matter what I decide.

☐ 262 HCN 5576   ☐ 462 HCN 5576

Name (please print)

Address   Apt. #

City   State/Province   Zip/Postal Code

Mail to the Harlequin Reader Service:
IN U.S.A.: P.O. Box 1341, Buffalo, NY 14240-8531
IN CANADA: P.O. Box 603, Fort Erie, Ontario L2A 5X3

Visit
ReaderService.com
Today!

As a valued member of the Harlequin Reader Service, you'll find these benefits and more at ReaderService.com:

- Try 2 free books from any series
- Access risk-free special offers
- View your account history & manage payments
- Browse the latest Bonus Bucks catalog